"Zandor," Alanna repeated under her breath in total incredulity. *Zandor?*

No, it couldn't be. Not possibly. She was nervous, so she'd misheard. That was all it was.

"I apologize, Grandmother. To you and my cousin's beautiful friend. We must all take care that no harm comes to her."

Not just the name, she thought dazedly. But the voice—low pitched and tinged with that same note of faint amusement. Instantly and hideously recognizable. Shockingly, horribly unmistakable.

As, God help her, she must be to him.

She forced herself to look up and meet the gaze of the tall figure, dark against the setting sun, framed in the French windows.

The man from whose bedroom she'd fled all those months ago, leaving her with memories that had haunted her ever since.

He closed the French windows behind him with elaborate care and strolled forward, broad shouldered, lean hipped, long legged in close-fitting black pants. His matching shirt was casually unbuttoned halfway to the waist, affording Alanna an unwanted view of his bronze chest, and an even more disturbing reminder that when she'd left his bed at their previous encounter, he'd been wearing no clothes at all.

He said softly, "Perhaps we should properly introduce ourselves. I am Zandor." He paused. "Zandor Varga, and you are...?"

Sara Craven is one of Harlequin/ Mills & Boon's most long-standing authors. Sadly she passed away on 15th November 2017. She leaves a fantastic legacy, having sold over 30 million books around the world. She published her first novel, *Garden of Dreams*, in 1975 and wrote for Mills & Boon/ Harlequin for over 40 years. *The Innocent's One-Night Confession* is her 93rd book.

Former journalist Sara also balanced her impressing writing career with winning the 1997 series of the UK TV show *Mastermind*, and standing as Chairman of the Romance Novelists' Association from 2011 to 2013.

Books by Sara Craven

Harlequin Presents

The Innocent's Shameful Secret
Inherited by Her Enemy
Seduction Never Lies
Count Valieri's Prisoner
The End of Her Innocence
His Untamed Innocent
The Innocent's Surrender
Ruthless Awakening

Seven Sexy Sins

The Innocent's Sinful Craving

The Untamed

The Highest Stakes of All

Visit the Author Profile page
at Harlequin.com for more titles.

Sara Craven

THE INNOCENT'S ONE-NIGHT CONFESSION

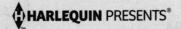

Recycling programs
for this product may
not exist in your area.

ISBN-13: 978-1-335-50433-3

The Innocent's One-Night Confession

First North American publication 2018

Copyright © 2018 by Sara Craven

Printed in U.S.A.

www.Harlequin.com

THE INNOCENT'S
ONE-NIGHT CONFESSION

For Leo, stern critic and amazing support.
Thank you for everything.

CHAPTER ONE

'So, come on, Becks. Tell all. What's he like in bed?'

Alanna Beckett nearly choked on her mouthful of St Clements as she cast an apprehensive glance round the crowded wine bar.

'Susie—for heaven's sake, keep your voice down. And you can't ask things like that.'

'But I just did,' said Susie, unruffled. 'I have a thirst for information that even this very nice wine can't satisfy. Think about it. I go to America for six whole weeks, leaving you alone in the flat and doing your usual imitation of a hermit crab. I come back terrified that you'll have adopted a cat, started wearing cameo brooches and signed up for an evening class in crochet—and, instead, you're on the brink of getting engaged. Hallelujah!'

'No,' Alanna protested. 'I'm not. Nothing like it. He's just invited me to his grandmother's eightieth birthday party. That's all.'

'An important family do at the important family house in the country. That's serious stuff, Becks. So, let's have some details about—Gerald, is it?'

'Gerard,' said Alanna. 'Gerard Harrington.'

'Also known as Gerry?'

'Not as far as I'm aware.'

'Ah.' Susie digested this. 'Complete physical description, warts and all?'

Alanna sighed. 'Just under six foot, good-looking, fair hair, blue eyes—and no warts.'

'As far as you're aware. How did you meet?'

'He saved me from being run over by a bus.'

'Good God,' Susie said blankly. 'Where—and how?'

'Not far from Bazaar Vert in the King's Road. I was thinking of something else and just—stepped off the pavement. He snatched me back.'

'Well, God bless him for that.' Susie stared at her. 'That's not like you, Becks. What on earth were you daydreaming about?'

Alanna shrugged. 'I thought I'd seen someone I knew.' She hesitated, thinking rapidly. 'Lindsay Merton, as a matter of fact.'

'Lindsay?' Susie repeated, puzzled. 'But she and her husband are living in Australia.'

'And I'm sure they still are,' Alanna returned brightly, cursing herself under her breath. 'So I nearly got squished for nothing.'

'What did Sir Galahad—aka Gerard—do then?'

'Well, I was naturally a bit shaky, so he took me into Bazaar Vert and got the manageress to make me some very sweet tea.' She shuddered. 'I'd almost have preferred being run over.'

'No you wouldn't,' Susie corrected briskly. 'Think of the unfortunate bus driver. And how come your knight errant has so much influence with the snooty ladies in Bazaar Vert?'

'Someone in his family—his cousin—owns the entire chain. Gerard is its managing director.'

'Wow,' said Susie. 'Therefore earning megabucks and ecologically minded as a bonus. Darling, I'm seriously impressed. Don't they say that if someone rescues you, then your life belongs to them for ever after?'

'"They", whoever they are, seem to say a lot of things, most of them plain silly,' Alanna returned evenly. 'And there's no question of belonging— on either side. Or not yet, anyway.' She shrugged. 'We're simply—getting acquainted. And this party is another step in the process.'

'Seeing if Grandma bestows the gold seal of approval?' Susie wrinkled her nose. 'Don't think I'd like that.'

'Well, it can work both ways. Anyway, it's a weekend in the country, so I intend to relax and just—go with the flow. Which will not carry me into sleeping with Gerard,' she added. 'In case you were wondering. It's strictly separate bedrooms at Whitestone Abbey.'

Susie grinned. 'With Vespers thrown in by the sound of it. But he might know where to find a convenient haystack.' She raised her glass. 'To you, my proud beauty. And may the weekend make all your dreams come true.'

Alanna smiled back and drank some more of her orange juice and bitter lemon. After all, she told herself, it might even happen.

And perhaps she could, at long last, dismiss her secret nightmare to well-deserved oblivion. Begin to live her life to the full without being crucified by memories of the private shame which had turned her into a self-appointed recluse.

Everyone made mistakes and it was ludicrous to have taken her own lapse so seriously. Even if it had been totally out of character, there'd certainly been no need to continue beating herself up about it, allowing it to poison her existence for month after dreary month.

'But why?' Susie had wailed so often. 'It's party time so forget your authors and their damned manuscripts for one evening and come with me. Everyone would be thrilled to see you. They ask about you all the time.'

And, invariably, her mind flinching, she'd used the excuse of work—deadlines—an increased list—and the very real talk of a possible takeover, to be followed, almost inevitably, by redundancies.

Explained, perfectly reasonably, that, to make sure of her job, she needed to put her heart and soul into her work. Which wasn't any real hardship because she loved it.

And, as reinforcement, she'd created this new office persona, quiet, dedicated and politely aloof.

Confined her cloud of dark auburn hair in a silver clasp at the nape of her neck. Stopped enhancing her green eyes and long lashes with shadow and mascara, restricting her use of cosmetics to a touch of lipstick so discreet it was almost invisible.

And only she knew the reason for adopting this deliberate camouflage. She hadn't even told Susie, best friend from school days and now flatmate, who'd provided her joyfully with the refuge she needed from her solitary bedsit, and was now equally delighted to welcome her apparent renaissance.

Not that she planned to abandon her current version of herself. She'd become used to it, telling herself that safe was far better than sorry. Not, of course, that she'd ever gone in for fashion's extremes or painted her face in stripes.

And Gerard seemed to like her the way she was, although she could, maybe, move up a gear without too much shock to his system.

Depending, she thought, on how things went at his grandmother's party.

The invitation had surprised her. Gerard was undeniably charming and attentive, but their relationship so far could quite definitely be characterised as restrained. Not that she had any objections to this. Quite the contrary, in fact.

She'd only agreed to have dinner with him on that first occasion because he'd put himself at risk to save her from serious injury at the very least, and it would have seemed churlish to refuse.

And, almost tentatively, she'd found herself relaxing and starting to enjoy a pleasant and undemanding evening in his company. It had been their third date before he'd kissed her goodnight—a light, unthreatening brush of his lips on hers.

Not, as Susie put it, a martini kiss. She'd been, to her relief, neither shaken nor stirred. At the same time, it was reassuring to reflect that she'd have no real objection to him kissing her again. And, when he did, to realise that she was beginning, warily, to find it enjoyable.

'We're going steady,' she'd told herself, faintly amused at the idea of an old-fashioned courtship, but thankful at the same time. 'And this time,' she'd added fervently, 'I'll get it right.'

All the same, she was aware that the coming weekend at Whitestone Abbey could prove a turning point in their relationship which she might not be ready for.

On the other hand, refusing the invitation might be an even bigger mistake.

On the strength of that, she'd spent a chunk of her savings on a dress, the lovely colour of a misty sea, slim-fitting and ankle length in alternating bands of silk and lace, demure enough, she thought, to please the most exacting grandmother, yet also subtly enhancing her slender curves in a way that Gerard might appreciate.

And which would take her through Saturday's cocktail party for friends and neighbours to the formal family dinner later in the evening.

'I hope you won't find it too dull,' Gerard said, adding ruefully, 'There was a time when Grandam would have danced the night away, but I think she's started to feel her age.'

'Grandam?' Alanna was intrigued. 'That has a wonderfully old-fashioned ring about it.'

He pulled a face. 'Actually, it was an accident. When I was away at school for the first time, she sent me a food parcel and when I wrote to thank her, I mixed up the last two letters of Grandma and it stuck.'

'Whatever,' she said. 'I think it's charming.'

'Well, don't think in terms of lavender and lace,' he said. 'She still goes out on her horse each day before breakfast, summer and winter.' He paused. 'Do you ride?'

'I did,' she said. 'Up to the time I left home to go to university and my parents decided to downsize to a cottage with a manageable garden, instead of a paddock with stabling.'

'Bring some boots,' he said, his surprised smile widening into a grin. 'We can fix you up with a hat and I'll give you a proper tour of the area.'

Alanna smiled back. 'That will be marvellous,'

she said, and meant it in spite of a growing conviction that the soon-to-be eighty-year-old Niamh Harrington was one formidable lady.

And then, of course, there was the rest of the family.

'Gerard's mother is a widow and his late father was Mrs Harrington's eldest child and only son,' she told Susie over a Thai takeaway at the flat that evening.

She counted on her fingers. 'Then there's his Aunt Caroline and Uncle Richard with their son and his wife, plus his Aunt Diana, her husband Maurice and their two daughters, one married, one single.'

'My God,' Susie said limply. 'I hope for your sake they wear name tags. Children?'

Alanna speared a prawn. 'Yes, but strictly with attendant nannies. I get the impression that Mrs Harrington doesn't approve of modern child-rearing methods.'

She added, 'She also had a third daughter, her youngest, called Marianne, but she and her husband are both dead, and their son apparently is not expected to attend the festivities.'

'Just as well,' said Susie. 'Sounds as if it will be standing room only as it is.' She paused. 'Is it this Marianne's son who owns Bazaar Vert?'

Alanna shrugged. 'I guess so. Gerard hasn't said much about him.' She picked up a foil dish. 'Share the rest of the sticky rice?'

'Willingly,' said Susie. 'But I'm glad to be missing out on the sticky weekend,' she added thoughtfully.

The stickiness, in fact, began early at the Friday morning acquisitions meeting.

Alanna walked from it into her cubbyhole of an office, kicked the door shut behind her and swore.

'Oh, Hetty,' she said quietly. 'Where are you when I need you?'

Well, on maternity leave was the answer to that, which was why Alanna had been temporarily promoted to head up romantic fiction at Hawkseye Publishing during her boss's absence.

Initially, she'd been thrilled at the opportunity, but now the rose-tinted spectacles were off and she realised she was in a war zone, the opposing foe being Louis Foster who produced the men's fiction list, mainly slanted towards the 'blood and guts' school of thought, but also including some literary names. And others, as Alanna had just found out.

She had gone to the meeting to sell a new author with a fresh voice and innovative approach, who was her own discovery.

She had spoken enthusiastically and persuasively about acquiring this burgeoning talent for the Hawkseye stable, only to find herself blocked by Louis's suave determination.

He could not, he said, having studied the figures, recommend such a high-risk investment in a total unknown.

'Especially,' he added, 'as Jeffrey Winton told me over lunch the other day that he was very keen to extend his range, and what he was suggesting sounds very similar to what this young lady of Alanna's is offering. And, of course, we'd have the Maisie McIntyre name which sells itself.'

Jeffrey Winton, thought Alanna, her toes curling inside her shoes, the bestselling creator, under a female pseudonym, of village sagas so sweet they made her teeth ache.

Also Hetty's author, so what the hell was he doing being wined and dined by Louis, let alone discussing future projects?

Not that she wanted to go within a mile of him, she thought, recoiling from the memory of her one and only encounter with the rotund, twinkling author of *Love at the Forge* and *Inn of Contentment*. And, even worse, what had followed...

Everything she had done her best to erase from her consciousness was now suddenly confronting her again in every detail, rendering her momentarily numb.

And while she was still faltering, Louis's powers of persuasion convinced the others round the table and she was faced with telling an author she believed in that there was no contract in the offing after all. Adding to her bitter disappointment twin blows to her negotiating skills and her pride.

And possibly moving Louis a definite step towards his ultimate goal of uniting men's and women's commercial fiction under his leadership.

All this, she thought wearily, and, in a few hours, her first encounter with the extended Harrington family, for which she probably needed all the confidence she could get.

She looked at her weekend case waiting in the corner, holding jeans and boots, together with the expensive tissue-wrapped dress and the handcrafted silver photograph frame she'd chosen as her hostess's birthday present.

For a moment she considered assuming the role of victim of a forty-eight-hour mystery virus, then dismissed it.

Having let her author down, she would not do the same to Gerard, mainly because she sensed he was anxious about the weekend too.

I must make sure it all goes well for his sake, she thought. And for the possibility of a future together—if and when liking grows into love.

A cautious beginning to a happy ending. The way it ought to be.

That was what she needed. Not a passionate tumultuous descent to guilt and the risk of disaster. That, like all other bad memories, must be locked—sealed away to await well-deserved oblivion.

Which would come, in spite of the recent unwanted reminder, she assured herself. It had to…

* * *

It was an uneventful journey, Gerard handling his supremely comfortable Mercedes with finesse while he chatted about the abbey and its turbulent history.

'It's said that the family who acquired it in Tudor times bribed the King's officials to turn the monks out and the abbot cursed them,' he said ruefully.

'Whether that's true or not, they certainly fell on hard times in later years, largely due to the drink and gambling problems of a succession of eldest sons, so my great-great-grandfather Augustus Harrington got it quite cheaply.

'Also being eminently respectable and hard-working, the restoration of Whitestone was his idea of recreation.'

'Is much of the original building left?' Alanna asked.

'Very little, apart from the cloisters. The Tudor lot simply pulled the whole thing down and started again.'

'Vandals.' She smiled at him. 'I suppose upkeep is an ongoing process.'

He was silent for a moment. 'Yes,' he said. 'Very much so. Maybe that's the real meaning of the abbot's curse. He said it would be a millstone round the owners' necks for evermore.'

'I don't think I believe in curses,' said Alanna. 'Anyway, even a millstone must be worth it—when it's such a piece of history.'

'I certainly believe that.' He spoke with a touch of bleakness. 'But that isn't a universal view. However you must judge for yourself.' He accelerated a little. 'We're nearly there.'

And he was right. As they crested the next hill, Alanna saw the solid mass of pale stone which was the abbey cradled in the valley below, its tall chimneys rearing towards the sky and the mullioned windows glinting in the early evening sunlight.

From either side of the main structure, two narrow wings jutted out, enclosing a large forecourt where a number of cars were already parked.

Like arms opening in welcome? Alanna wondered. Well, she would soon find out.

Gerard slotted the Merc between a Jaguar and an Audi, just to the right of the shallow stone steps leading up to the front entrance. As she waited for him to retrieve their luggage from the boot, Alanna saw that the heavily timbered door was opening, and that a grey-haired woman in a smart red dress had appeared, shading her eyes as she watched their approach.

'So there you are,' she said with something of a snap. She turned to the tall man who had followed her out. 'Richard, go and tell Mother that Gerard has arrived at last.'

'And good evening to you too, Aunt Caroline.' Gerard's smile was courteous. 'Don't worry, Uncle Rich. I can announce us.'

'But you were expected over an hour ago.' His aunt pursed her lips as she led the way into an impressive wainscoted hall. 'I've no idea how this will affect the timing of dinner.'

'I imagine it will be served exactly when Grandam ordered, just as usual,' Gerard returned, unruffled. 'Now, let me introduce Alanna Beckett to you. Darling—my aunt and uncle, Mr and Mrs Healey.'

Slightly thrown by the unexpected endearment, Alanna shook hands and murmured politely.

'Everyone is waiting in the drawing room,' said Mrs Healey. 'Leave your case there, Miss—er—Beckett. The housekeeper will take it up to your room.' She turned to Gerard. 'We've had to make a last change to the arrangements, so your guest is now in the east wing, just along from Joanne.' She gave Alanna a dubious look. 'I'm afraid you'll have to share a bathroom.'

'I'm used to it.' Alanna tried a pleasant smile. 'I share a flat in London.'

Mrs Healey absorbed the information without comment and returned to Gerard. 'Now do come along. You know how your grandmother hates to be kept waiting.'

It occurred to Alanna as she followed in Mrs Healey's wake that she wasn't really ready for this. That she would have preferred to accompany her case upstairs and freshen up before entering the presence of the Harrington matriarch.

Or—preferably—return to London, on foot if necessary.

Gerard bent towards her. 'Don't worry about Aunt Caroline,' he whispered. 'Since my mother went off to live in Suffolk, she's been taking her role as daughter of the house rather too seriously.'

She forced a smile. 'She made me wonder if I should curtsy.'

He took her hand. 'You'll be fine, I promise you.'

She found herself in a long, low-ceilinged room with a vast stone fireplace at one end, big enough, she supposed, to roast an ox, if anyone had an urge to do so.

The furnishings, mainly large squashy sofas and deep armchairs, all upholstered in faded chintz, made no claim to be shabby chic. Like the elderly rugs on the dark oak floorboards and the green damask curtains that framed the wide French windows, they were just—shabby.

A real home, she acknowledged with relief, and full of people, all of whom had, rather disturbingly, fallen silent as soon as she and Gerard walked in.

Feeling desperately self-conscious, she wished they'd start chatting again, if only to muffle the sound of her heels on the wooden floor, and disguise the fact that they were staring at her as Gerard steered her across the room towards his grandmother.

She'd anticipated an older version of Mrs Healey,

a forbidding presence enthroned at a slight distance from her obedient family, and was bracing herself accordingly.

But Niamh Harrington was small and plump with bright blue eyes, pink cheeks and a quantity of snowy hair arranged on top of her head like a cottage loaf in danger of collapse.

She was seated in the middle of the largest sofa, facing the open windows, still talking animatedly to the blonde girl beside her, but she broke off at Gerard's approach.

'Dearest boy.' She lifted a smiling face for his kiss. 'So, this is your lovely girl.'

The twinkling gaze swept over Alanna in an assessment as shrewd as it was comprehensive, and, for a moment, she had an absurd impulse to step back, as if getting out of range.

Then Mrs Harrington's smile widened. 'Well, isn't this just grand. Welcome to Whitestone, my dear.'

The distinct Irish accent was something else Alanna hadn't expected although she supposed 'Niamh' should have supplied a clue.

She pulled herself together. 'Thank you for inviting me, Mrs Harrington. You—you have a very beautiful home.'

Oh, God, she thought. Did that sound as if she was sizing the place up for future occupancy? And had Gerard warned his grandmother that they'd only been dating for a few weeks rather than months.

Mrs Harrington made a deprecating gesture with a heavily beringed hand. 'Ah, well, it's seen better days.' She turned to the girl beside her. 'Move up, Joanne darling and let—Alanna, is it?—sit beside me while she tells me all about herself.'

Gerard was looking round. 'I don't see my mother.'

'Poor Meg's upstairs having a bit of a lie down. I expect she found the journey from Suffolk a great burden to her as I always feared she would.' Mrs Harrington sighed deeply. 'Leave her be for now, dearest boy, and I'm sure she'll be fine, just fine by dinner.'

Alanna saw Gerard's mouth tighten, but he said nothing as he turned away.

'So,' said Mrs Harrington. 'My grandson tells me you're a publisher.'

'An editor in women's commercial fiction.' Alanna knew how stilted that must sound.

'Now that's a job I envy you for. There's nothing I love more than a book. A good story with plenty of meat in it and not too sentimental. Maybe, now, you could suggest a few titles that I'd enjoy.'

'Can you recommend a book for an elderly lady who loves reading?'

Almost the same request she'd heard in a London bookshop nearly a year ago, but spoken then in a man's deep drawl. And the start of the nightmare she needed so badly to forget, she thought, trying to repress an instinctive shiver.

Which was noticed. 'You're feeling cold and no wonder, now the evening breeze has got up.' Niamh Harrington raised her voice. 'Will you come in now, Zandor? And close those windows behind you, for the Lord's sake. There's a terrible draught, and we can't have Gerard's guest catching her death because you're wandering about on the terrace.'

Alanna found she was freezing in reality. She stared down at her hands, clasped so tightly in her lap that the knuckles were turning white.

'Zandor,' she repeated under her breath in total incredulity. *Zandor?*

No, it couldn't be. Not possibly. She was nervous so she'd misheard. That's all it was.

'I apologise, Grandmother. To you and my cousin's beautiful friend. We must all take care that no harm comes to her.'

Not just the name, she thought dazedly. But the voice—low-pitched and tinged with that same note of faint amusement. Instantly and hideously recognisable. Shockingly, horribly unmistakable.

As, God help her, she must be to him.

She forced herself to look up and meet the gaze of the tall figure, dark against the setting sun, framed in the French windows.

The man from whose bedroom she'd fled all those months ago, leaving her with memories that had haunted her ever since.

And for the worst of all possible reasons.

CHAPTER TWO

HE CLOSED THE French windows behind him with elaborate care and strolled forward, broad-shouldered, lean-hipped, long-legged in close-fitting black pants, his matching shirt casually unbuttoned halfway to the waist, affording Alanna an unwanted view of his bronze chest, and an even more disturbing reminder that, when she'd left his bed at their previous encounter, he'd been wearing no clothes at all.

He said softly, 'Perhaps we should properly introduce ourselves. I am Zandor.' He paused. 'Zandor Varga, and you are…?'

She produced a voice from somewhere. A husky travesty of her usual clear tones. 'Alanna,' she said, and swallowed. 'Alanna Beckett.'

He nodded, those astonishing, never forgotten pale grey eyes studying her, hard as burnished steel.

'It is a delight to meet you, Miss Beckett…' He paused, and she swallowed, waiting for him to say 'again' and for the questions to begin.

His faint smile told her he had read her thoughts. He said silkily, 'But then my cousin Gerard has always had exquisite taste.' And turned away.

She felt limp with relief, but knew that was only transitory. That she was by no means off the hook.

And that the day which had started badly had just got a hundred—a thousand times worse.

She realised now that it hadn't been her imagination playing tricks that day in Chelsea. That as the owner of the Bazaar Vert chain, he'd been visiting the King's Road branch and must have just left when she caught that brief but dangerous glimpse of him. And that Gerard had been seeing him off the premises when he came to her rescue.

It was also apparent, from Gerard's passing remarks and his aunt's irritable comment about last minute changes, that Zandor had indeed not been expected at the birthday celebrations.

Oh, God, she thought, panic clawing at her. If only he'd stayed away…

And wondered why he'd changed his mind.

But even so, they'd have been bound to meet eventually, that is if she went on seeing Gerard. And how could she—under the circumstances? When that night with Zandor would always be there, a time bomb lethally ticking its way down to disaster.

Because the way he'd looked at her had told her quite plainly that he was not simply going to let bygones be bygones.

Presumably her hasty and unheralded departure had offended his masculine pride. That he was usually the one to walk away. Well, tough. She owed him nothing, as she would make clear when the time inevitably came.

However, Mrs Harrington could not have detected anything amiss in the recent exchange as her lilting tones had reverted to the subject of books.

'*Middlemarch*, now,' she was saying. 'Did you ever read that? A wonderful book, but what a fool young Dorothea to be marrying that dried-up stick of a man. And then leaping out of the frying pan into the fire with the other fellow.' She snorted. 'A ne'er do well, if ever there was one. And what in the world is it that draws a decent girl to the likes of them?'

Somehow, Alanna managed a smile. 'I've no idea. But it's still a great novel.'

As I told your grandson who bought it for you around this time last year...

She was grateful when they were interrupted by Mrs Healey.

'Isn't it time we all got ready for dinner, Mama? I know we're not actually *dressing* tonight, but I'm sure Miss Becket, for one, would like to tidy herself,' she added with a look suggesting that Alanna had recently been dragged through a hedge backwards. 'Joanne can show her to her room.'

Alanna found her hand being patted. 'I have to let you go, dear girl,' said Niamh Harrington. 'But there'll be plenty of time for another grand chat.'

Joanne turned out to be the blonde who'd been sitting beside her grandmother, not just pretty but clearly disposed to be friendly.

'Rather you than me for the cosy chats,' she confided as they went upstairs. 'Grandam has a way of asking questions when she already knows the answers. But that won't happen with you.'

Oh, God, I hope not, thought Alanna, her heart sinking.

'And you know about literature,' Joanne went on. 'It's as much as I can do to get through *Hello!* in the hairdresser's, and Kate's as bad, although she can use Mark and the baby as an excuse for being too busy to read.'

At the top of the impressive stone staircase, she turned left. 'We're down here—spinsters' alley, I suppose, although you don't really qualify as you and Gerard are an item.'

'It's a bit early to call it that,' Alanna said carefully. 'We've only been going out together for a few weeks.'

'But he's brought you here. Exposed you to the entire Harrington onslaught.' Joanne giggled, naughtily. 'I bet Grandam gave you the full once-over, checking for childbearing hips. Her father owned a stud farm in Tipperary, and she practically claims to be descended from Brian Boru, so she'll want to know all about your family—suitable blood lines and all that. No dodgy branches on the family tree.'

Alanna gasped. 'You are joking.'

'Not altogether.' Joanne pulled a face. 'She does

take the whole thing horribly seriously, and I've never had a boyfriend I've dared bring here in case he turns out to be spavined or sway-backed or something equally ghastly.'

She opened a door. 'Well, this is you. I hope you'll be comfortable,' she added dubiously. 'The bathroom's between us. It's only small, because it used to be a powdering room for people's wigs, but the water's always boiling, and there's a door into the bedrooms on each side which we can bolt, so no need to sing loudly during occupancy.'

She looked at her watch. 'I'll be back to collect you in forty minutes. Will that do?'

Alanna could only nod.

Left alone, she sank down on to the edge of a rather hard mattress on a three-quarter-size bed, and looked around her. It was an old-fashioned room with a narrow window, and made even darker by cumbersome furniture dating from the beginning of the previous century, and wallpaper covered in flamboyant cabbage roses in a shade of pink Nature had overlooked.

Her bag had been placed on the foot of the bed, so she unfastened it and extracted tomorrow evening's dress, removing its tissue paper wrapping before hanging it in the cavernous wardrobe.

Joanne, she decided, was undoubtedly indiscreet as well as cheerful, and she would probably need to be on her guard. But the other girl could be a valuable source of information and a few casual questions could do no harm.

Because it was clear that Niamh Harrington's other grandson, whose arrival for her birthday party had caused such a disturbance to the arrangements as well as destroying her own peace of mind, was also something of an outsider.

Her first instinct was, once again, to run. To invent some work-related emergency involving an imperative summons back to London. But that would, quite correctly, lead Zandor Varga to suppose she was scared of him, and what was left of her pride forbade it.

Besides, the Harrington family *en masse* now seemed more of an advantage than a problem. By the time she'd done the rounds and met them all, it should be perfectly possible to lose herself among them, thus avoiding any further contact with Zandor.

And, of course, Gerard would be her shield too, she told herself, wondering why that was an afterthought.

Her immediate dilemma was what to wear that evening. She'd brought a dress, of course, a black, knee-length linen shift. It wasn't the one she'd been wearing when she first met Zandor—that had been consigned to the dustbin the following day—but it bore far too distinct a resemblance to the other for her comfort. On the other hand, she felt hot and sticky in the clothes she'd travelled in, and her skirt was badly creased.

I'll just have to bite on the bullet, she thought. Brazen the situation out. Let him think what he likes.

Her decision made, she took a quick refreshing bath in the deep, old-fashioned tub, then dressed swiftly and brushed her hair till it shone. She clasped a necklace composed of flat silver discs round her throat adding a matching bracelet to her wrist.

She disguised her unwelcome pallor with a discreet use of blusher and masked the strained lines of her mouth with a brownish-pink lipstick.

She reached for her scent spray, then hesitated. She only ever wore one perfume—Azalea, from the distinctive Earth Scents range by Lizbeth Lane, a new young designer whose workshop she'd visited with Susie when she first arrived in London.

And that was something he would definitely recognise—if he got close enough, she thought, sudden heat pervading her body as she returned the atomiser to her makeup purse.

She was trying to calm herself with some Yoga-style breathing when Joanne tapped on her door.

'Ready for the lions' den?' she asked cheerfully. 'You certainly look great. Your hair is the most amazing colour—rather like Gran's antique mahogany dining table. Granny Dennison, I mean, not Grandam.'

'You call her that too?'

'We all do,' Joanne said as they walked to the stairs. 'Except Zan, of course. He sticks to the formal Grandmother when he visits—which isn't that often.'

She sighed. 'None of us knew he was coming this time either. I suppose it's about money again, which means the usual row. And unfair, I think, to put her in a bate on her birthday weekend. On the other hand, I guess we must be thankful he didn't bring Lili.'

She encountered Alanna's questioning look and flushed scarlet. 'Oh, hell, me and my big mouth. Look, just forget I mentioned her—please.'

'Forgotten,' Alanna assured her over-brightly, reflecting she'd been entirely accurate about Joanne's talent for indiscretion.

But it was interesting that the dynamic, all-conquering Mr Varga needed money, suggesting that Bazaar Vert might be feeling the economic crunch along with other high-profile businesses.

Gerard had mentioned nothing about any downward turn, but she could hardly expect that he would, any more than she'd confessed to him her fears about the takeover at Hawkseye, now said to be looming. They weren't on those sorts of terms.

And now they never would be, which might be disappointing, but hardly the end of the world.

It would have been far worse if she and Gerard

had become seriously involved before she discovered his cousin's identity.

It occurred to her that earlier there'd been a tension between the pair of them that was almost palpable, so perhaps the financial difficulties were all too real.

However, that was none of her business, and in forty-eight hours it would all be over anyway. And she'd be free to get on with the rest of her life.

And there was no need to wonder about Lili. She would simply be Zandor's latest choice to share his bed. And welcome to him.

Even if his trading figures were down, his rapid turnover in willing women would undoubtedly be continuing unabated. It was probably only his grandmother's strict embargo on extra-marital sex that had prevented him from bringing her as his guest.

And why the hell am I sparing the situation even a moment's thought anyway? Alanna asked herself savagely as they reached the drawing room.

Although she knew the answer to that. Zandor's re-emergence into her life had thrown her completely. She felt as if she'd gone sailing on a calm lake, under a blue sky, only to find herself helpless and at the mercy of a squall that had come out of nowhere.

Oh, get a grip, she thought with sudden impatience.

Certainly Zandor had not been pleased when they met earlier, but maybe her own sense of shock had made her read too much into his reaction. By now, he'd surely have had time to think. To realise their previous encounter had been a long time ago, and that they had both moved on.

At least that was how she planned to handle things from now on, until the weekend was safely over. And, hopefully, for ever after.

'So there you are, sweetheart.' Gerard came to meet her and, drawing her towards him, gave her a long, lingering kiss on her astonished mouth.

As he raised his head Alanna stepped back, aware that she was blushing, not with pleasure but with embarrassment and more than a touch of anger at this second demonstration of totally uncharacteristic behaviour.

The words 'What on earth...?' were already forming when she looked past him and saw, a few yards away, Zandor watching them, silver eyes glittering in a face that looked as if it had been hacked from dark stone.

And instantly she swallowed the tart query, tossing back her hair and forcing her lips into the semblance of a flirtatious smile instead, aware as she did so that Zandor was turning abruptly and walking away.

Now do your worst, she sent after him in silent defiance.

Gerard took her hand. 'Come and say hello to my mother,' he invited.

'Is she feeling better?' Alanna's tone was stilted, conscious as they crossed the room that covert glances and shrugs were being exchanged as if Gerard's family were as surprised by the kiss as herself.

'There was never anything the matter with her.' Gerard's smile was rueful. 'She and Grandam have always had something of an edgy relationship, so she finds headaches useful.'

'Oh,' was the only reply Alanna could conjure up. It occurred to her that Whitestone Abbey seemed to harbour all kinds of other tensions at various levels.

A pleasant weekend in the country? she thought drily. Not by any stretch of the imagination.

Meg Harrington was ensconced in an armchair, slim and elegant in white silk trousers and a loose shirt in shades of blue, rust and gold. Her fair hair, skilfully highlighted, was cut in a smooth, expensive bob, and her makeup was flawless.

She gave Alanna a polite, faintly puzzled smile as Gerard performed the introduction, then picked up an empty highball glass from the table beside her chair and held it out to him. 'Get me a refill, would you, honey?'

'I didn't know my son was bringing a friend,' Mrs Harrington said as he departed on his errand. 'Have you known each other long, Miss—er—Beckett?'

Saying, 'Oh, call me Alanna, please,' seemed strangely inappropriate, so she contented herself with, 'Just a few weeks, actually.'

The other woman's brows lifted. 'And you agreed to accompany him here? How incredibly brave of you.'

Alanna shrugged. 'I'm an only child, so I find a large family gathering like this tremendously appealing.' She paused, hoping the lie didn't sound as ridiculous as it felt, then aimed for something approaching the truth. 'Gerard's grandmother has been very welcoming.'

Meg Harrington said drily, 'I don't doubt it.'

'And the house is amazing,' Alanna added with spurious brightness. 'Such an interesting history.'

'A white elephant,' said Gerard's mother. 'In the last stages of decay. I couldn't wait to leave. And here comes my drink.'

But not brought by Gerard.

'Drowning your sorrows, Aunt Meg?' Zandor enquired pleasantly as he handed her the glass.

'Anaesthetising them, certainly. And wondering what other surprises are in store.' She paused. 'I presume you're here alone?'

His mouth tightened. 'Of course. And for business rather than pleasure.'

'Nothing new there then. I wish you luck.' She raised her glass. 'Cheers. Now why don't you get a drink for Gerard's new friend, here.' She sounded amused. 'The poor child looks as if she needs one.'

'No,' Alanna said quickly. 'Thank you. I'm fine—really.'

She turned and walked away, only to find Zandor at her side and keeping pace with her.

He said softly, 'Running away again, Alanna?'

She stared rigidly ahead of her, angrily aware that her heartbeat had quickened and she was blushing. 'Just looking for Gerard, as it happens.'

'And hoping for another loving reunion, no doubt.' He sounded faintly amused. 'However, he's been summoned to the book room to have a private word with Grandmother Niamh. They won't wish to be interrupted.' He paused. 'So why don't I get us both a drink and take them on to the terrace for our own quiet chat? I think we should have one, don't you?'

She took a deep breath. 'On the contrary, we have nothing to discuss,' she said icily. 'And I don't drink any more—at least not alcohol. I'm sure I don't have to explain my reasons.'

He said slowly, 'Actually, yes, I think you do. That is if it relates in some way to our previous encounter. If you're implying you ended up in bed with me because you were drunk.'

'Good guess.' She clenched her shaking hands into fists at her sides. 'And my first mistake. Fortunately not fatal.'

'Hardly,' he said. 'After a couple of glasses of champagne. I'd have called it—pleasantly relaxing.'

'I'm sure you would.' She added tautly, 'And that's all I have to say, so now, please, leave me alone.'

'Just as you left me?' His tone bit. 'But I have done so, my sweet, for almost a year, and—do you know?—I have discovered that it no longer pleases me. Especially now that I have seen you again—and under such interesting circumstances.'

His smile did not reach his eyes. 'And before you think of another stinging retort, remember that this room is filled with people who believe we met for the first time today and might wonder why we are so soon on bad terms.'

'On the other hand,' she said. 'From what I gather, you seem to make a habit of upsetting people.'

He said quietly, 'Then, by all means, go on gathering. You may collect a few surprises on the way. But, understand this. One day—or night—we will have that chat. So be ready.'

And he walked away, leaving her standing there, those words 'be ready' beating in her brain, and drying her mouth.

She turned precipitately towards the door, impelled by a frantic need to be alone. To think…

Only to find herself being intercepted by Joanne.

'Has Zan been coming on to you?' Her tone was anxious. 'My God, he's the screaming limit. He must have women dotted all over the known world, and then some, so he has no right—no right at all.' She added earnestly, 'Honestly, Alanna, you don't want to believe a word he says.'

'Don't worry.' Joanne had just confirmed that she'd allowed herself to be used for a night's amusement by a serial womaniser, yet Alanna managed to summon a smile from somewhere. 'I won't.'

'Anyway,' Joanne added more buoyantly. 'You're Gerard's girl—right?'

Wrong, thought Alanna. The truth is I don't really know at this moment who I am or what I'm doing here, but the weight of opinion seems to tend towards past fool and present fraud. But for now…

She lifted her chin. 'Absolutely right,' she said clearly.

'And my parents are dying to meet you.' Joanne guided her across the room. 'But don't worry,' she added cheerfully. 'Mother and Aunt Caroline are chalk and cheese. You'd never think they were sisters.'

Mrs Dennison was a comfortably built lady whose greeting was as warm as her smile.

'Well, you've been thrown in at the deep end,' she said cheerfully, motioning Alanna to sit beside her. 'You're not seeing us at our best, I fear, but please don't blame Gerard. He wasn't to know how things would turn out.' She turned to her husband. 'And now it seems my mother's invited Tom Bradham tomorrow evening. Just asking for more trouble.'

Maurice Dennison shrugged. 'Something she thrives on, darling. So relax, and let Caroline fret about the seating arrangements.' He glanced at his watch. 'It's almost time for dinner, so I'd better detach Kate and Mark from the nursery and frog-march them downstairs.'

'My mother,' said Diana Dennison, as he walked away, 'must be the only great-grandmother in the world who still believes that little children should be seen—briefly—but not heard. So they get to come down from the nursery once a day at teatime. Accordingly that's why their parents choose to spend the greater part of their time upstairs with them.'

She sighed. 'Mark's parents would have the boys like a shot, and they'd have a wonderful time on the farm, yet Mother always insists on them being brought here when she issues a family summons.' She shook her head. 'I can never understand why. She's never been fond of children—not even her own if memory serves,' she added drily.

She gave Alanna another smile. 'I've shocked you, haven't I? But Gerard won't mind you knowing how things are.'

More information, Alanna thought, that I could well do without.

She said carefully, 'I think I should make it clear that I haven't actually known Gerard for very long.'

Mrs Dennison shrugged. 'He can't be too concerned about that, or he wouldn't have invited you,' she returned calmly. 'And I'm delighted he did. I intend to tell my nephew that he's a fool if he lets you slip away.'

Alanna was agonised. 'Mrs Dennison—please...'

The older woman sighed again. 'I'm sorry, but I'm fond of Gerard and I want to see him happy again. However, if it means so much to you, I won't say a word.' Her smile was suddenly mischievous. 'Let nature take its course.'

Not, thought Alanna, a course of action with any appeal for me.

Mrs Dennison paused. 'And here comes my sister, looking rattled. I suppose that means that Mother is now waiting for us all in the dining room, tapping her foot impatiently. Let's not keep her waiting any longer.'

It was a long and leisurely meal which turned out to be less of a nightmare than Alanna expected. For one thing, the food was excellent and, for another, she found herself sitting at the far end of the table, a long way from Gerard and, thankfully, even further from Zandor.

Her immediate neighbours were Desmond Healey, a quiet, humorous replica of his father, and his pretty wife, both of them drama buffs. And, for a while, she managed to lose herself in a light-hearted argument about TV *noir* and if the Scandinavians still led the field or had been overtaken by the French and Italians.

When the meal was over, it was late enough for her to be able to excuse herself politely from the return to the drawing room, a swift glance having assured her that Zandor was nowhere to be seen, claiming mendaciously that coffee kept her awake but adding truthfully it had been a very long day.

She'd noticed that Niamh Harrington was also missing and that Gerard had disappeared again too, presumably to continue their earlier conference, so she was able to escape up to her room without any further unwonted and public demonstrations of affection from him.

No wonder people were thinking their relationship was a done deal, she thought, closing her door and, for reasons she was unable to explain, turning its heavy key in the old-fashioned lock.

She found Mrs Dennison's comment about wishing to see Gerard 'happy again' buzzing in her brain as she got ready for bed.

I've never seen any sign that he's been miserable, she mused, with an inward shrug. Although perhaps having to work for his cousin might be getting him down, which raised the question why he'd accepted a job in the first place from someone who was clearly *persona non grata* with the rest of the family.

It's beyond me, she decided as she switched off

the lamp. And also not my problem. Not that it ever was or ever would be.

She drew back the curtains to admit the moonlight, and tried to get comfortable on a mattress that she discovered was lumpy as well as hard.

She was almost asleep when she heard the soft knock at the door. She propped herself on an elbow staring across the room and saw in the half-light the handle slowly turn.

She stayed silent, motionless, until it returned to its original position followed by quiet footsteps receding down the passage.

He'd gone—and she didn't even have to question the identity of her late-night visitor.

As she lay down, she realised she'd also been holding her breath.

That key, she told herself, will go everywhere with me until I finally walk out of here on Sunday morning. And say goodbye to the Harrington family for ever.

CHAPTER THREE

ALANNA WOKE VERY early the next morning, aware that she'd spent a restless night in the grip of dreams she was glad not to remember too clearly.

She slid out of bed and crossed to the window, only to find any view of the gardens was obscured by a thick cloud of mist hanging like a pall at tree level.

Towards the east, however, the sky was vermilion shot with flame, promising another hot day. And perhaps more, she thought, remembering an old saying from childhood, 'Red sky in the morning, sailors' warning' which suggested storms in the offing.

As if there hadn't been enough already, she thought, shivering a little as she pulled on the lawn wrap which matched her white nightdress, before curling up on the thinly cushioned seat under the window.

She should never have agreed to come here, she told herself. Quite apart from the nightmare of finding herself face to face with Zandor again, her visit had obviously raised expectations in Gerard's family about their relationship which were as premature as they were embarrassing. And which were now, in any case, due to be totally disappointed.

And was that her own reaction too?

In all honesty, she didn't know. Couldn't even begin to consider all the might-have-beens that were now denied her.

Not when she had to deal with the reality of Zandor and his ongoing disruption of her life and her peace of mind.

Which had all begun, she recalled wretchedly, with a 'Meet the Reader' event, starring the loathsome Jeffrey Winton. And her feet hurting…

Alanna discreetly eased off one high-heeled pump and flexed her toes. These were not standing-about-in shoes, she reflected ruefully, but having her stand beside him instead of sit at the table was Jeffrey's idea, and certainly not hers.

Nor had it been her plan to spend this Friday evening in a bookshop, listening to him talk about his life, his writing career, primarily his incarnation as Maisie McIntyre, and his future plans to a crowd of adoring women fans.

Clearly no one had ever told him that self-praise was no recommendation.

Izzy, the Hawkseye Publishing publicist scheduled to accompany him, had gone home during the afternoon with a migraine, and Alanna had been the only one around when Hetty came looking for a replacement.

Her protests had been ignored. 'Sometimes, it's all hands to the pump,' Hetty had decreed. 'It's simple enough. He just needs someone to pass him the books to be signed and keep the queue moving. Oh, and he prefers smart dress for his back-up,' she added flicking a glance at Alanna's jeans, T-shirt and trainers. 'Including shoes.

'Also he tends to sign all the books we send so that the shop can't return them, so fend him off because the owner of SolBooks doesn't like it.'

Now, nearly an hour into Mr Winton's description of how he'd learned to get in touch with his feminine side in order to write about the whimsical and endearing events in his rural sagas, Alanna had murder in her heart.

Back at her bedsit, she had scripts to read and report on, music to listen to, a bowl of soup followed by a jacket potato smothered in cheese to enjoy and an elderly but comfortable robe to wear.

Instead, she was stranded here in her one and only little black dress and some toe-crushing footwear.

She wished that someone would stand up and ask, 'What do you say to the rumours that your wife writes over fifty per cent of your books?' but of course it didn't happen.

His audience, whose tickets included a glass of wine, had completely bought into the Maisie McIntyre dream world, and they were hooked—mesmerised, and almost panting to get their hands on the piles of *Summer at the Shepherd's Crook* that shop-owner Clive Solomon was bringing from the stockroom.

'This will be my last Meet the Author session,' he'd confided when she arrived. 'I'm retiring, and handing the business over to my nephew as both my daughters are married and sublimely uninterested in bookselling. I shall keep my hand in with a spot of antiquarian dealing on the internet,' he added with satisfaction.

And Alanna, wishing that he'd had a more congenial writer at his swansong, smiled and wished him every success.

She was just squeezing her protesting foot back into her shoe when she realised that there was a new arrival in the shop, who'd apparently just pushed open the door and walked in off the street. And that unlike the rest of the rapt crowd, he was male.

He was also tall, very dark, his thin face striking rather than conventionally handsome, and elegantly clad in a charcoal grey suit, his immaculate white shirt set off by a crimson silk tie.

So hardly, she thought, a journalist who'd also been sent there on an unwilling mission.

Just someone in the wrong place at the wrong time.

As she walked down the shop towards him, she was aware too that he was looking back at her. That his grey eyes, so pale they were almost silver, with their colour enhanced by long black eyelashes, were conducting a leisurely and comprehensive survey of her that she should have resented.

Also that his firm-lipped mouth was beginning to quirk into a smile. To which, she discovered to her own astonishment, she was sorely tempted to respond.

She said quietly but firmly, 'I'm afraid this is a private book launch. Or do you have a ticket?'

'No.' He glanced round him. 'I thought the shop was having a late-night opening. As I'm here, can you recommend a book for an elderly lady who loves to read?'

She hesitated. Mr Solomon was still busy, and Jeffrey Winton was looking daggers in her direction, so the obvious answer was to advise this potential customer to return another time. Except he wouldn't. He'd buy elsewhere and she liked Mr Solomon and didn't want him to miss out on a sale.

'What sort of thing does she like?'

'Good stories with plenty of characters, I understand.' He looked past her, frowning faintly. 'Is he an author?' he asked quietly.

'Yes,' Alanna whispered. 'But I don't think he'd be her choice.' She paused. 'Has she read *Middlemarch* by George Eliot?'

'I haven't the faintest idea. Did you enjoy it?'

'It's one of my all-time favourites.'

'Then you have a sale.' His smile was glinting

in those astonishing eyes, and prompting a strange and unfamiliar tremor deep within her.

'I'll leave that to Mr Solomon,' she said hurriedly, seeing that he was heading enquiringly in their direction. 'I need to get back to my author.'

He said softly, 'To my infinite regret,' and she felt her face warm as she hurried back to the table.

During the applause at the end of the talk, she permitted herself a quick glance towards the door, but the stranger had gone, and she found herself suppressing a pang of disappointment.

The signing session went well, although Alanna did not appreciate Mr Winton's unctuous reference to herself as 'my lovely helper' or his insistence on her moving nearer to his chair, when her preference was for keeping her distance.

She'd already noticed with faint unease his sideways glances at the length of her skirt, the depth of her neckline and the way the fabric clung to the gentle curves in between.

She was thankful when the queue began to dwindle and people started to take their reluctant departures. Clive Solomon was already collecting the used glasses and she, remembering Hetty's warning, decided to add some extra tape to the unopened cartons in the stockroom, in case Mr Winton decided to pull a fast one.

And next time Maisie McIntyre has a book

launch, I'll be the one claiming a migraine, she thought grimly, if not a brain tumour.

She picked up the tape and started work, glad it was a mindless occupation because her brain seemed for some reason to be working on images of a man with a slanting smile and silver eyes.

So much so that she didn't even realise she had company until Jeffrey Winton spoke.

'That's rather naughty of you, my dear. You should be promoting my sales, not obstructing them.'

She straightened. 'I think all the customers have gone, Mr Winton,' she returned, wishing he was not standing between her and the door, and that Clive Solomon wasn't packing up the unused wine in his tiny staffroom.

'But a whole lot of new ones will be in the shop tomorrow.' His tone was jovially reproving as he took a step closer. 'However, you're young and I might be persuaded not to report you to Hetty.'

'And a fat lot of good that would do you,' Alanna said under her breath as she stepped backwards, only to find herself trapped between his bulky body and the steel shelving.

Oh, God, she thought in horror, please don't let this be happening. Please...

'That is,' he added, 'if you're prepared to be nice to me.'

He licked already moist pink lips expectantly,

leering at her as he moved closer, his hand snaking towards the hem of her dress.

What, Alanna wondered wildly, would be the penalty for kneeing a bestselling author in the groin?

But before she could take the risk, another voice intervened.

'Haven't you finished yet, darling?' He was back, the customer, the silver-eyed focus of her recent imaginings, leaning casually in the doorway, smiling at her and ignoring Jeffrey Winton who had spun round, red-faced and furious at the interruption. 'You promised me the rest of the evening— remember?'

She said huskily, 'I'm quite ready. I—I just need my jacket and bag.'

She eased past Mr Winton and collected her things from the staffroom, uttering a few words of breathless congratulation on a successful evening to Mr Solomon before joining her unexpected rescuer at the shop door.

'It seems I arrived at the right moment,' he commented helping her into her jacket.

'Yes,' she said with a shudder. 'I still can't really believe it.' She took a deep breath. 'I—I don't know how to thank you.' She paused. 'But what made you come back? Did you change your mind about the book?'

'No,' he said. 'I wanted to ask you to have dinner with me.'

She hesitated, feeling her pulses quicken outrageously. 'That's very kind of you,' she managed. 'But truly, there's no need.'

'I disagree,' he said. 'For one thing, I'm keen to continue our discussion of English literature. Also I dislike eating alone.'

'But I don't even know your name…'

'It's Zandor,' he said. 'Or Zan, if you prefer. And you are…?'

She swallowed. 'Alanna.'

'So now we are at least fifty per cent respectable,' he said. 'The rest can wait.'

As he signalled to the cab that had suddenly appeared from nowhere, it occurred to her that by no stretch of the imagination could she accept that solitary dining would ever play a major role in his life.

From the moment she'd seen him, she'd recognised that he was a seriously attractive man on a scale marking as dangerous, at the same time registering an exhilarating awareness that her blood seemed to be flowing more quickly. That her senses had somehow become more finely tuned.

Knowing at the same time that by accepting his invitation, she could be making a disastrous leap from a hot frying pan into a raging inferno.

A view reinforced by the sight of Jeffrey Winton emerging from SolBooks and glaring venomously in her direction. Proof, if proof were needed, that he was unlikely to be a good loser, she thought, her stomach churning with renewed alarm, as she shrank into her corner of the cab.

Which Zan noticed as he took his seat beside her.

'What's the matter?'

She said shakily, 'I'm sorry, but I'm not very hungry. I—I'd like to go home, please.'

'Do you live with your family?'

'No, I have a flat.' An absurdly upbeat way, she thought, to describe one room with a kitchen alcove, and a shared bathroom.

'Which you share?'

'Well—no.'

He nodded. 'Then I think our original plan is best.' His tone was matter-of-fact. 'You've had an unpleasant experience but some food and company will help put it behind you. Solitary brooding will not.'

'That's easy for you to say,' she flashed back. 'You don't stand to lose your job over this evening's fiasco. Jeffrey Winton is a huge bestseller. If he spins some yarn about me, guess who will be believed?'

He frowned. 'I could speak to your boss. Tell him what I saw. He seems a guy who would listen to reason.'

But my boss is a woman. She has to consider the bottom line... The words were trembling on her lips, but she swallowed them unspoken.

Zan, she realised, must think she worked at Sol-Books, and, on the whole, that seemed preferable to launching into complicated explanations about her junior role at Hawkseye. Or any other personal detail, for that matter.

And she felt too weary to go on arguing about dinner. For one thing, the planned soup and jacket potato no longer held the slightest appeal for her. And he was trying to be kind, so she could at least be civil in return for an hour or so.

Besides, she owed him—didn't she?

After that—well, they would be ships that passed in the night. Nothing more, she decided, staring out of the window at the brightly lit shops—which suddenly seemed oddly blurred.

And realised to her horror that she was crying, quietly and unstoppably.

She heard Zandor say something under his breath, and found herself drawn towards him. She gave herself up the astonishing comfort of being cradled in his arms, her head against his shoulder. Of breathing the warm scent of his skin and the faint but heady fragrance of his cologne. And, not least, the sheer practicality of having an immaculate linen handkerchief pushed into her hand.

'He was so vile.' She sobbed the words into his expensive tailoring. 'If you hadn't been there—if you hadn't come back…'

'Hush,' he whispered, his hand gently and rhythmically stroking her hair. 'It's over. You're safe now.'

And she'd believed him, she thought. Had cried

herself out while he held her, then sat up awkwardly, reducing his handkerchief to a sodden lump as she blotted her eyes and blew her nose.

'I feel so stupid,' she said huskily.

'There's no need.' He pushed a strand of damp hair back from her forehead and she felt the brush of his fingers resonate through every inch of her skin.

At the same time she realised the cab was coming to a halt and, as Zandor paid the driver, found herself standing outside an imposing facade announcing itself as the Metro-Imperial Hotel, with a uniformed commissionaire holding open a pair of elegant glass doors.

As they crossed the expanse of marble-tiled foyer towards a bank of lifts, Alanna hung back.

'Why are we here?'

'To have dinner.' He urged her forward gently, his hand under her elbow. 'I didn't have time to book a table anywhere else. But the food is good.'

And then she was in the lift, which was rising smoothly and swiftly past floor after floor until it reached the very top.

'Is this the restaurant?'

'No, the penthouse. I stay here when I'm in London.' He unlocked the door straight ahead of them with his key card and ushered her into a sitting room, all pale golden wood and ivory leather sofas with enough space to accommodate her bedsit twice over and then some.

He pointed to a door on the far wall. 'You might want to freshen up. Go through there and you'll find the bathroom's directly opposite.' He paused. 'Do you like pasta?'

'Well—yes,' she admitted uncertainly.

'Good.' He smiled at her. 'Then that's what we'll have.'

'Through there' was, of course, the bedroom, also huge and with a bed vast enough for several kings plus an emperor, Alanna thought as she headed for the bathroom, the imperial note being continued in the deep purple quilted bedspread.

Apart from a two-tier wooden stand bearing an opulent leather suitcase, open and neatly packed, the bed was the only visible piece of furniture, so presumably the wardrobes and chests of drawers were concealed behind the room's elegant cream panelling.

The bathroom with its walk-in shower and sunken tub was lavishly supplied with soft towels and toiletries, and one glance in the mirror above the twin marble washbasins at her red-eyed, tear-stained reflection revealed to Alanna how essential the freshening up process was and why a public restaurant might not have been her companion's immediate choice.

Or his second, she discovered, when, all signs of her recent distress removed and her makeup discreetly renewed, she returned to the sitting room and found a waiter laying places for two at a table beside the long windows while another was busy with a gold-foiled bottle and an ice bucket.

Zandor was lounging on a sofa, jacket removed, tie loosened, and the top buttons of his shirt unfastened. His attention was fixed frowningly on the laptop on the low table in front of him, but he closed it at her approach and smiled up at her.

'Did that help?'

'Amazingly so.' She sat down beside him, but at a discreet distance, and took another longer look around her. 'This is—palatial.'

He shrugged. 'It does the job while I'm in London. Right now, I seem to spend most of my time on aircraft. Tomorrow I'm heading off to the States.'

Which explained the waiting suitcase.

'You enjoy travelling?'

'It doesn't worry me.' His mouth twisted. 'But then I've always been regarded as having gipsy blood.'

'How—exciting.' She'd almost said 'romantic' but stopped herself just in time.

He said drily, 'Except it's never been intended as a compliment.'

She was wondering how to respond to this when she was diverted by the waiter's arrival with two flutes of pale wine, fizzing with bubbles.

'Champagne?' She drew a breath. 'But why?'

He shrugged. 'You think it's just for celebrations? It isn't. Tonight, treat it simply as the world's best tonic.'

She accepted the flute uncertainly. 'Well—thank you.'

'We should have a toast.' He touched his glass lightly to hers. 'Health and happiness.'

She repeated the words softly and drank.

The cool, dry wine seemed to burst, fizzing, in her mouth, caressing her throat as she swallowed.

She said with a little gasp. 'You're right. It's wonderful.'

And the food which arrived shortly afterwards was just as good—fillets of salmon wrapped in prosciutto, served on a bed of creamy tarragon pasta with asparagus, peas and tiny broad beans.

The dessert was a platter of little filo pastry tartlets filled with an assortment of fruits in brandied syrup.

All of it enhanced accompanied by the chilled sparkle of the champagne.

And by conversation, starting with books and moving on to music, quiet, entertaining, and always involving, so that, in spite of her initial forebodings, Alanna found she was relaxing into enjoyment. Savouring his company almost more than the delicious supper.

Yet, at the same time, becoming increasingly aware of the potency of his attraction. How his slow smile and the quiet intensity of his silver gaze made her nerve-endings quiver and set her pulses racing—reactions which bewildered as much as they disturbed her.

She wasn't a child for heaven's sake. She'd enjoyed a satisfactory social life at university and since her arrival in London. But liking had not so far ripened into passion and none of the young men she'd dated had ever come close to persuading her into a more intimate relationship.

That, she'd told herself, was because casual relationships had little appeal for her, and, anyway, she was far more interested in concentrating her emotional energy on the development of her career.

Or was it just because she'd never been seriously tempted to abandon her self-imposed celibacy.

Not that she was now, of course, she added hastily.

And, thankfully, the evening would soon be over, and no harm done.

After all, the conversation, however enjoyable, had remained strictly impersonal. They hadn't even exchanged surnames, she reminded herself, which made it very much a 'ships that pass in the night' occasion.

And she should put out of her mind the sense of comfort and security she'd experienced in the taxi when he'd held her in his arms as she wept. Once again, he was just being kind. Nothing more. And far better—safer—to believe that.

The arrival of the coffee, however, prompted a move back to the sofa. And it had also, she realised, signalled the departure of the serving staff, leaving them alone together.

She made a thing of looking at her watch. 'Heavens, I didn't realise how late it was. I should be leaving. I—I've already taken up too much of your time.'

'I think we both know that isn't true.' He paused, then added, 'Have some coffee,' filling one of the small cups from the tall silver pot. 'Then I'll call the desk and order a cab for you.'

As he passed her the cup, their fingers brushed and she felt the brief contact shiver through her senses.

It was so quiet in the room that it seemed the swift uneven pounding of her heart must be audible to them both.

She pushed back a strand of hair from her forehead and saw him watching the swift, nervous movement of her hand and stared down, trying to calm herself, concentrating her attention on the dark swirl of coffee in her cup.

She thought, This is madness...

When she'd finished the last rich drop, she returned her cup to the tray.

She said too brightly, 'That was delicious. But now I really must be on my way.'

'Of course,' he said, and picked up the telephone.

He gave the order for the taxi and listened, nodding, to the response.

'It may be a few minutes,' he said, as he replaced the receiver. 'Apparently it has begun to rain.'

'That doesn't matter,' she said quickly, rising to her feet and reaching for her jacket and bag. 'I—I'll wait in the foyer. There's no need for you to come down.'

His brows lifted but all he said was, 'As you wish.'

At the door, Alanna turned. 'Thank you again—for everything,' she said and held out her hand.

But instead of the brief handshake she'd expected, Zan's fingers closed round hers, carrying them to his lips and kissing them gently.

At her sharp indrawn breath, he paused, smiling down into her widening eyes, then turned her hand, letting his mouth caress the soft hollow of her palm.

Sensations began to uncurl inside her—pleasure and a kind of yearning that she had not experienced before but which she found strangely, even dangerously, beguiling.

So much so that when he took her in his arms, she went unresistingly, swaying against his body, feeling herself enveloped by the heat of his skin, as if the layers of clothing between them had ceased to exist.

His hands tangled in her hair, framing her face as he brought her mouth to his. As his lips slowly, almost wonderingly, explored the contours of hers, then coaxed them apart to allow the dark, sweet invasion of his tongue.

As she yielded—responded—to this new intimacy, she found her hands gripping his shoulders as if they were her only security in a suddenly reeling world, where her legs seemed no longer able to support her.

Their mouths clung, as his kisses deepened from gentleness to urgency and an open hunger that she could neither ignore nor deny because she shared it.

Even when she realised his fingers were releasing the zip on her dress and pulling the loosened fabric from her shoulders, she made no protest, melting into him as his lips caressed a slow path down her throat.

She was absorbed, lost in bewilderment—in the soft, hot ache of desire—when the sudden insistence of the telephone ringing intruded violently, like a whiplash across her senses.

Zan said something under his breath and released her, striding across to the phone, responding to the caller with a curt 'Very well' before replacing the receiver.

He looked back at Alanna. 'Your taxi is here.'

Even without that, the brief interruption had been enough, bringing her starkly back to the reality of what she was inviting. And telling her that it must end.

She said shakily, 'Yes—yes, of course.'

Clumsily, she pulled her dress into place and closed the zip, then reached down for her bag and jacket which had slipped from her grasp to the floor.

Zan came back to her side as she was fumbling with the door handle.

He said laconically, 'There's a trick to it,' and demonstrated.

'Yes, I see now.' She forced a smile. 'Well— goodnight.'

'Wait.' His voice was husky. 'Don't leave.'

'I—I must...'

'No.' He stared down at her, the silver eyes brooding. 'Let me send the cab away.' He drew a harsh breath. 'Oh, God, Alanna. Stay with me tonight. Sleep with me.'

'I—can't.' She looked away, fixing her gaze on the open door and the empty corridor beyond it. 'I—I don't—I've never...' She was stumbling over her words, embarrassed at what she was revealing. 'Please—let me go.'

There was a pause, then he said quietly, 'If that's what you want,' and stood aside to let her pass.

She walked the few yards to the lift, trying not to run. Instinct telling her that he was still there, watching her from the doorway.

And, even as she pressed the button for descent, found she was whispering over and over again under her breath, 'Don't look back—don't look back...'

CHAPTER FOUR

AND THEN...

No, Alanna told herself almost violently. Nothing more. I will not—*not* go there. Never again.

Chilled and cramped, she found she'd almost curled into a ball, her arms wrapped protectively round her body, and straightened slowly, inwardly cursing her own stupidity at allowing past mistakes to impinge on her again.

On the other hand, she argued to herself, it could have been very much worse. Supposing Zandor had spent this weekend elsewhere, as he'd clearly been expected to do, and she'd remained in ignorance of his connection to the Harringtons. She might well have found herself embarking, if tentatively, on a serious relationship with Gerard.

Imagine, she thought, her mouth twisting, how that would have crashed and burned when I eventually discovered the truth, and that particular skeleton came tumbling out of the woodwork.

As it is, I can ease myself out of the situation, with no broken bones—alive or dead.

A knock at the door brought her to her feet. 'Who is it?' She kept her voice steady.

'Joanne. I have coffee, if you don't mind black without sugar.'

'Sounds great.' She crossed to the door, the key grating in the lock as she turned it.

Joanne, a steaming mug in either hand, gave her an astonished look. 'You're safety conscious,' she commented. 'If you're worried about the abbot's ghost, it's only supposed to haunt the cloisters.'

'I didn't even know it existed,' Alanna returned, waving Joanne towards the only chair before she returned to the window seat with her own coffee. 'And aren't ghosts supposed to walk straight through doors and walls anyway?' She hesitated. 'But I guess locking myself in is a habit dating from my bedsit days.'

Joanne giggled naughtily. 'Poor Gerard, if he risked Grandam's eagle eye to come visiting.'

Alanna forced a smile in return. 'No, the rules were explained to me in advance.'

And if anyone dared to ignore them, it certainly wouldn't be Gerard, she thought, her throat tightening. Just someone who was strictly a law unto himself.

'Well the pair of you must make sure you get some time alone today and prepare yourselves for this evening. Repeating silently that it will all be over by this time tomorrow works for me.'

Alanna looked at her, this time with genuine amusement. 'Joanne—that's absurd. It's just a birthday party.'

Joanne sighed. 'It's never "just" anything with Grandam. Witness her invitation to Lord Bradham.'

Alanna remembered Mrs Dennison had mentioned the name with foreboding.

'Don't you like him?' she asked.

'He's lovely. Local landowner. Very rich. Life peer for services to conservation.'

'Then what's the problem?'

'Ah, so Gerard hasn't told you.' Joanne pulled a face. She lowered her voice. 'The problem is that he was engaged to my aunt Marianne. Date fixed and everything. She went off to Paris to stay with her godmother who was buying her wedding dress, and was invited to some party at the embassy. One of the other guests was a guy called Timon Varga. A bit of a mystery man with plenty of looks and charm, but a bit short on background.

'A week later, Marianne walked out of the house with her passport, and the wedding dress which had been delivered the day before, leaving a note to say she was marrying this glamorous unknown.'

She rolled her eyes. 'Naturally, all hell broke loose. I mean—a week for God's sake. She must have been meeting him on the sly, but no one had suspected a thing.'

She shook her head. 'Grandam was raving that he was nothing but a con man and a gipsy who thought Marianne had money, and she wanted to start a police hunt, but Grandfather talked her out of it. He said Marianne was over eighteen and free to choose for herself, however mistakenly that might be.

'And if Grandam was right and she did come back abandoned, destitute and pregnant, they would look after her.'

'What about her fiancé?' Alanna asked. 'How on earth did they tell him?'

'They didn't have to. Marianne had already written to him apparently. Naturally, he was desperately upset—so much so, he closed up his house and went off to Canada. When he came back two years later he was also married—to a girl called Denise that he'd met in Montreal.'

She gave a sudden giggle. 'Grandam loathed her on sight, and when he got his life peerage and Denise became Lady Bradham, she was fit to be tied, muttering it should have been Marianne.'

Alanna cleared her throat. 'Who was not, presumably, abandoned and destitute?'

'Far from it,' said Joanne. 'When Grandfather insisted they should be invited down to the abbey, my mother says Marianne was wearing a diamond like the Rock of Gibraltar. It turned out that her husband was absolutely loaded and that they adored each other.

'Grandam, of course, wouldn't accept that. She did her damnedest to find out where he came from and how he'd made his money, but she never did, so she told the rest of the family, he must have bad blood and was probably a criminal of some kind and Marianne would be lucky if he didn't end up in jail with her alongside him.'

Alanna almost choked on her coffee. 'How could she?'

'Quite easily. After Zan was born, Ma says she used to refer to him as the gipsy brat, even when he was old enough to understand.'

'I...see,' Alanna said slowly.

'Anyway, that's why Lord Bradham, who's now a widower, has suddenly been invited. To remind Zan that, to Grandam, he's still an outsider and that's the man his mother should have married.' She paused rather awkwardly. 'Among other things.'

So much for the smiley, white haired old lady, thought Alanna.

She finished her drink and handed Joanne the empty mug. 'Thank you for that.'

'No problem. When Gerard brings you down here without the rest of us, shove a kettle and a jar of instant in your bag. The kitchen's out of bounds before breakfast which is served at nine o'clock sharp.' She winked. 'Another company rule.'

Alanna forced another smile. 'I'll remember.'

And not just the coffee...

She now had even more reason to ease herself out of the situation, she thought, as she took her shirt, jeans and boots from her bag. The sun was out now and most of the mist had dispersed, so presumably she and Gerard would be going riding and spending the rest of Saturday as planned.

Maybe as Joanne had said, remembering her stay would be over in twenty-four hours might work for her too.

And when they were back in London, she could tell Gerard that she felt things were not working out between them.

And wished she felt more disappointed.

Niamh Harrington was presiding at the breakfast table, still in her riding breeches and silky polo-necked sweater, plus pink-cheeked and twinkly-eyed, even though neither her daughter-in-law nor Zandor had observed the nine o'clock deadline. For which Alanna had to be thankful.

She had politely wished Mrs Harrington a simple 'Many happy returns of the day' as Gerard told her that gifts would be presented at dinner that evening, and helped herself to toast and coffee from the sideboard.

'So, dear girl, you ride, do you?' her hostess inquired briskly as Alanna sat down. 'I wish I'd known. You could have come out with me earlier.'

Alanna, staring down at the tablecloth, murmured that she hadn't been on a horse for some time.

'No matter.' Niamh dismissed that with a wave of her hand. 'We'll put you on Dolly. She's quiet and easy paced.

You'll be fine.' She paused, her brow wrinkled. 'And I could always call Felicity. I'm sure she'd be glad to ride over and keep you company.'

Alanna became aware that all other conversation at the table had suddenly ceased.

The silence was broken by Gerard. He said evenly, 'There's no need for that, Grandam. I expect Felicity has plenty to do. Anyway, I'm taking Alanna riding.'

'But not this morning, darling.' She gave him a tranquil smile. 'Didn't I say I wanted you to ride over to the Home Farm for a chat with Mr Hodson? It must have slipped my mind, but he'll be expecting you.'

She paused. 'But you're probably right about Felicity. After all, it's little enough her father sees of her these days, poor man.'

Alanna saw Joanne and her mother exchanging glances, and hurried into speech.

'Gerard, I honestly don't mind about the riding. I can explore the cloister and have a wander round the gardens instead.'

'No, no,' said Mrs Harrington. 'A good canter in the fresh air will do you more good. Put some colour in your face instead of that pale London look.'

She nodded. 'I'll tell Jacko, my groom, to go along with you and make sure you don't get lost.' And returned to her boiled egg.

Alanna, her cheeks burning, decided bitterly she need no longer worry about her pallor.

If Mrs Harrington was delivering a message that she was out of place here, it was quite unnecessary. And so she would tell Gerard as soon as the first opportunity presented itself. In fact her immediate impulse was to request him to drive her to the nearest station and a train back to London, and to hell with the party, the abbey, and everyone in it.

Except, of course, that Zandor might draw the conclusion that this unexpected departure had some connection with him, and that was something her pride could not risk.

No, she decided grimly, she would stick it out to the bitter end.

Her breakfast finished, she excused herself politely and left the dining room. Gerard, tight-lipped and his eyes stormy, halted her at the foot of the stairs.

'Where are you going?'

'To change.' She indicated her jeans and boots. 'I've decided to save your grandmother's groom the trouble after all and spend the morning here.'

'No,' he said urgently. 'I must talk to you—and privately. So, I'm going to ride over to the Home Farm and while I'm down at the stables I'll tell Jacko to take you up to Whitemoor Common, and join you as soon as I've finished with old Hodson.'

Alanna hesitated. 'Do you think that's wise?'

'I think it's essential.' He paused. 'Is it agreed?'

She sighed. 'I suppose—yes.'

After all, she reasoned as she continued to her room, this time to fetch a sweater, this private talk could work both ways.

Dolly was a dapple grey, sturdy rather than elegant, but with a calm eye and Jacko was on much the same lines, watching critically as Alanna swung herself into the saddle and rode beside him out of the yard and along the track beside the paddock.

He was also a man of few words. 'Whitemoor Common, is it, miss?' and her response of, 'Yes, please,' being the sum total of their conversation.

Fifteen minutes along a quiet lane brought them to their destination, a wide expanse of scrubby grassland and bracken, studded with pale rocks and the occasional tree.

Jacko gave her a brusque nod and turned his own horse back towards the abbey.

Alanna watched him go, then dismounted, hitching Dolly's reins over a low branch of a mountain ash. Removing her borrowed hat, she pulled off her sweater, tying it loosely over her shoulders, before seating herself on the short grass at the side of the lane, her back against a white painted stone, announcing 'Whitemoor' in faded black letters, and lifting her face to the sun while Dolly cropped contentedly a few feet away.

All in all, she thought, a pretty isolated spot, but she knew that Gerard had set off for Home Farm over an hour before, so maybe she would not have to wait too long.

Nor did she. The warmth was just beginning to make her feel drowsy after her restless night when Dolly gave a soft whinny.

Alanna opened her eyes and sat upright, as she saw a solitary rider on a stylish bay cantering slowly towards her from the opposite side of the common.

It occurred to her, watching his approach, that Gerard was a much better horseman than she would have supposed. But then, she chided herself, what possible justification did she have for making such a judgement about him—apart from his seeming perfectly at home in the city?

Yet, she thought as she got to her feet, lifting a hand to shade her eyes, he was also the heir to the abbey.

Except…

She drew a swift, sharp breath.

Except, now that she was no longer dazzled by the sun, she could see that the new arrival not only had hair as dark and glossy as a raven's wing, but was also wearing a deep crimson shirt as opposed to the blue that Gerard had been wearing at breakfast. And knew exactly who was getting closer by the second.

To this isolated spot—her own assessment— where every instinct was warning her that it would be too dangerous to be alone with him.

I won't, she thought. Dear God, I *can't*...

Her mouth was suddenly dry, her heart thundering in panic as she stumbled towards Dolly, unhitching her reins with a jerk, then hurling herself up into the saddle and recklessly kicking the startled mare into a gallop.

She heard him shout her name, but ignored it, bending low over Dolly's neck and urging her on, her breath sobbing in her throat, realising too late that the treacherously uneven surface of the common was the last place to stage any kind of race.

Because Zandor was coming after her. Gaining on her fast, even though Dolly, rudely jolted out of her normal placidity, was now making a fight of it with her stablemate, leaving Alanna to curse her own stupidity.

She tried to pull on the reins, but the mare tossed her head in protest and tore them from her grasp, leaving her clinging desperately to Dolly's mane.

At the same moment, Zandor drew level with them. He reached an arm across and snatched Alanna from her saddle, his iron grip pinning her to his side and leaving her dangling helplessly as he brought his own horse under control and then to a complete halt.

Alanna began to struggle. She said breathlessly, 'Let go of me, damn you. Put me down.'

'With pleasure,' he returned curtly and dropped her, letting her land on her backside on a tussock of coarse grass with a thud that seemed to jar every bone in her body.

Dolly had slowed too, and was trotting in bewildered circles, apparently realising that the unexpected excitement was over.

Zandor patted his horse's neck, murmuring something soothing in a language Alanna did not recognise, then dismounted looping his reins round the branch of a small stunted tree, then walked over to Dolly, whistling softly.

At first she shied away, then as he waited, still whistling the same quiet tune, she dropped her head and came to him, allowing him to walk her back and tether her near the bay.

Meanwhile, Alanna, her breathing still flurried, had scrambled ungracefully to her feet, swearing under her breath, as she resisted the need to rub her aching rear.

Zandor observed her, tight-lipped. He said icily, 'Next time you wish to risk your neck, try jumping off a tall building. Dolly may be past her best, but she doesn't deserve to end her days with a broken leg or worse.'

He added, 'I understood you could ride. Don't you know better than to gallop headlong over unknown country?

'Especially as there's marshy ground ahead? And you aren't wearing a hat.'

The honest answer was 'Yes, of course I do.'

But Alanna didn't return it. Instead, she lifted a defiant chin. 'I had a hat but I left it at the roadside. What are you doing here?'

'I came to find you.' He paused. 'I'm aware you were expecting my cousin, but he will not be joining you after all.'

'How did you know that?' she asked sharply.

'I was in the stableyard when he was talking to Jacko. So, too, was our grandmother, who had other commissions for him after his visit to the Home Farm.' He gave her a thin smile. 'So I decided to save you a long, futile wait in the sun.'

Alanna bit her lip. 'Please don't expect me to be grateful.'

'I don't.' Zandor shrugged. 'Besides I also thought it would be a golden opportunity for us to have that talk I promised.'

'We have nothing to talk about.'

He said quietly, 'There, once again, we must differ.' His gaze was steady, the silver eyes intent, making her aware that her sweater had slipped off during that mad, ludicrous dash and that her sweat-dampened shirt was clinging revealingly to her body, emphasising the swell of her rounded breasts. An additional humiliation, she realised angrily.

'Let us go back to the first time you ran away from me,' Zandor went on. 'When I woke up to find you gone without a word—then or later.'

He paused. 'What the hell did I do to warrant that?

Because I really need to know.'

Her throat was dry. 'I suppose your usual conquests hang around begging for more. Let's just say I turned out to be the exception to the rule.'

He said harshly, 'And that's a cheap retort which insults us both.'

'We had a one night stand.' It was her turn to shrug, struggling to keep her voice casual. 'No big deal.'

'Again, I don't agree.' His voice took on a purr of intimacy. 'Shall I go through my reasons?'

'No!' In spite of herself, the negation seemed to explode from her and she hastily tempered it with, 'Thank you.' She spread her hands. 'It—it was all a long time ago.'

'To me, it still seems like yesterday.'

'Then that's your problem.' She swallowed. 'Why can't you let the past stay exactly that instead of raking over old mistakes?'

She added defensively, 'After all, it's not going to make the slightest difference—to either of us.'

He was silent for a long moment, his expression

unreadable. He said, 'Then let us turn our attention to the future and allow me to offer you a word of warning.' He paused. 'You and Gerard?' He shook his head. 'It's never going to happen. You would be well advised to walk away.'

The obvious and truthful response was 'I couldn't agree more,' she thought, stiffening. But that was her decision, not his. And, anyway, what right did he have to interfere—either to warn or advise?

She said coolly, 'My relationship with Gerard is a private matter for us alone.'

'Not any longer,' he said, his mouth twisting. 'And certainly not in this family. They invented the words "public domain".'

'Then let me tell you they've all been very kind and—welcoming.'

'Does that "all" include Aunt Meg and Aunt Caroline?' He raised an ironic eyebrow. 'Or my grandmother, for that matter?'

Her hesitation was fractional. 'She's been—charming.'

'Why not? She has bundles of it when she chooses. She sometimes even uses it on me. But that makes no difference to her long-term plans for Gerard, which do not, my lovely one, include you, I can promise you.'

'Please don't call me that,' she said tautly. 'And Gerard's future is his own to decide and he may consider I have a role to play in it.'

'Then why isn't he here with you now, finding some quiet, sheltered place and getting you out of your clothes?'

As she stared at him, shocked, he added, 'Or is that not yet part of the agenda?'

Alanna threw back her head. She said chokingly, 'How—how dare you? That's none of your business.'

'But it's very much my concern.' Zandor's voice slowed to a drawl. 'Having initiated you into the pleasures of physical passion, my sweet, I wouldn't wish you to feel—short-changed in any way.'

Alanna pressed her hands to her burning face. 'I don't,' she said defiantly. 'In any way.'

Which, she told herself, was no more than the truth—if not in the way he expected.

She added, 'I trust you don't want details.'

He was unfazed. 'Thank you but I think I prefer my memories.'

He let that sink in. Sting.

'So Niamh is charming and Gerard attentive,' he went on musingly. 'But don't let that fool you. If you're also thinking long term, Gerard can't afford to get married.'

'You're his employer,' she flashed. 'Perhaps you should pay him more.'

'Perhaps I would,' he said, 'if I was more convinced about his commitment to Bazaar Vert.'

He paused. 'However, his present salary already

allows him a very pleasant flat in Chiswick, his car, and an expensive boat currently moored at Chichester, plus his New Year skiing trips, and his summer vacations in the Caribbean, as I'm sure you're fully aware,' he added silkily. 'All of which hardly puts him on the breadline.'

Alanna bit her lip. 'And as he's also aware, I'm not exactly on the breadline myself,' she mentioned crisply.

'No, you work in publishing, for a company called Hawkseye,' he said slowly. 'And not as an assistant in a bookshop as I once thought.'

'Does it matter? They're both perfectly respectable occupations.'

'Yes,' he said. 'But unless you've also won millions in the Euro lottery, neither of them equips you financially to be the wife of the heir to Whitestone Abbey.'

He continued drily, 'Unless, of course, you're prepared to take on Niamh and convince him he needs that particular destiny like a hole in the head.

'To do that, you'd need to be either very brave or very reckless. And while you certainly don't lack the second trait, you may not come off unscathed again. Not a third time.'

'A third?'

'Why, yes,' he said. 'The first was the night at my hotel when you let the taxi I'd ordered leave without you.' He added unsmilingly, 'Or had you forgotten that small but important detail?'

The silence stretched between them as Alanna tried to think of something to say. And failed.

As if she had spoken, Zandor nodded. 'What I need to know is—why? Or are you going to use the champagne as your excuse again?'

The words bit at her. She made herself meet his gaze. 'No—although I've never drunk very much alcohol.'

Perhaps because I've seen where it can lead...

She went on, 'Perhaps I was simply—curious. I'd come to realise I was something of an anomaly in this day and age and maybe I wanted to—know what I was missing.'

'And, on a whim, chose me for this daring experiment?' His voice was harsh. 'Please don't expect me to be grateful.'

'I don't.' She stumbled on. 'I—I soon realised I'd committed a terrible—an unforgivable error. That it was the last thing I wanted to happen. I—I couldn't face you—afterwards—so I—left.'

His eyes were as bleak as winter. 'It didn't occur to you to tell me much earlier—maybe when it started—that you'd changed your mind? That you wanted it all to stop?'

'Oh, sure,' she said bitterly. 'And you've have accepted that. Patted me on the head and said "That's fine. Don't worry about it." I read about cases like that all the time in the papers.'

'Of course,' he said, with equal bitterness. 'And it was somehow simpler to include me with all the brainless louts who won't take no for an answer.'

She swallowed. 'Zan…'

'No,' he said almost violently. 'You don't call me that. Not now. Not ever again.'

'I don't understand…'

'You don't have to. Just believe that it's—safer.' Shaken, Alanna watched him draw a deep breath. Regain his control.

When he spoke again, his tone was dry. 'After all, you might make another mistake and use it in front of Gerard. Make him—wonder just how well-acquainted we really are.' He paused. 'Unless, that is, you've already told him.'

'No,' she said, still on edge. 'Why would I want to admit that I'm damaged goods?'

She saw his mouth tighten and braced herself. But all he said was, 'Why indeed?'

He became brisk. 'Now it's time you went back to the abbey before my grandmother thinks of any other little tasks to keep Gerard occupied and out of reach for the rest of the day.

'If you turn right by those boulders, you'll find an easy track that will take you almost straight to the stables—unless you decide on another gallop.'

He unhitched Dolly and led her over.

'But don't hope for too much,' he went on as Alanna mounted and settled herself in the saddle, trying not to wince. 'Whether you're damaged goods or pure as the driven snow, it makes no difference. He's still not for you.'

'Thank you,' she said. 'I'll decide that for myself.'

'Which,' he said softly, 'could be another terrible mistake. You seem prone to them.'

He untied his own horse and swung himself lithely into the saddle.

She said sharply, 'I can find my own way. You don't need to accompany me.'

'I wouldn't dream of it,' he returned. 'I'm merely going to retrieve the expensive hat you abandoned earlier.' He paused. 'Unless, of course, you want to give my grandmother additional ammunition.'

He gave her a mocking salute and rode off.

She watched him go, then slowly turned Dolly for home, grateful that the mare seemed happy to resume her usual staid pace.

But even more thankful, she thought, that Zandor would never know the truth.

And felt the tears she dared not shed burn like acid in her throat.

CHAPTER FIVE

THE RETURN TO the abbey was more of an amble than a ride. Dolly clearly would have known the way blindfold and Alanna, struggling to subdue her inner turmoil, was content, even grateful, to let the mare take charge, and allow her to think.

The important—the *only*—thing was, had Zandor believed her? Had their previous encounter now been dealt with and laid to rest?

And as she reviewed endlessly everything that had been said, she could start to believe that it had. That it was finally finished. And for that she had to be thankful.

She was recalled to the present by Dolly's soft whicker as the roofs of the stables came into view, reminding her that she had other problems to attend to.

It seemed her resolve to proceed with caution in her relationship with Gerard had been the right one. Certainly if she'd been allowing herself to fall in love with him, she'd now be devastated.

Not, she reminded herself hastily, that Zandor's warnings were necessarily valid. The strange dynamics of the Harrington clan alone might well have caused him to adopt his own agenda.

On the other hand, she could see that the abbey

clearly needed an injection of seriously hard cash, which she, the daughter of a country solicitor, would never be able to provide, even if she'd felt so inclined.

Because the abbey, she suspected, could well be a bottomless pit.

She was also realising that she'd probably totally misinterpreted Joanne's comments about potential clashes over money during the weekend. Because the family history she'd subsequently heard indicated that it would not be Zandor—the gipsy, the outsider—asking his grandmother for financial help, as she'd assumed, but quite the other way round.

Not, she thought, a happy state of affairs.

However, from a purely selfish point of view, no business of hers. And something else she could soon put behind her altogether.

But at least this interlude with Gerard had been enjoyable enough to bring her permanently out of her self-imposed seclusion. In future, she'd be as much of a social animal as even Susie could wish.

And one day she might find herself involved in a real relationship. Something to hope for, anyway, she thought, sternly stifling the odd pang twisting inside her.

She was in Dolly's stall, removing her saddle, when Jacko appeared.

'You'd best leave that to me, and get yourself up

to the house' he said gruffly. 'The Missus is asking for you.'

Well, the Missus could wait, Alanna decided, relinquishing Dolly reluctantly, at least until she'd soothed in a hot bath the last of the aches and pains from being summarily dumped on the common, and put on some clothes free of mud and grass stains.

She let herself into the house by the side entrance and was just crossing the hall to the stairs when she was intercepted by the housekeeper, Mrs Jackson.

'Oh, you're back, Miss Beckett. That's good. Mrs Harrington has been waiting for you to join her for coffee in the library.'

A note in her voice told Alanna unequivocally that this was not a suggestion but a command that she would do well to obey.

Reluctantly, she followed Mrs Jackson to the unexpected and unwanted rendezvous.

It wasn't a large room, and the oak shelving that covered three of its walls from floor to ceiling, filled with leather bound tomes that Alanna could bet were never opened from one year to the next, made it seem smaller and darker, making her glad she wasn't claustrophobic.

The fourth wall was occupied by an ornate fireplace, its grate, at this time of year, filled with an attractive arrangement of dried flowers.

Two high-backed leather armchairs, a coffee table between them, confronted each other on either side of the hearth, and Niamh Harrington, predictably, Alanna thought sourly, was seated in the one facing the door.

Since breakfast, she'd changed into a silk caftan in sapphire blue, embroidered with butterflies.

'So here you are at last!' she exclaimed. 'I was becoming anxious, dear girl, when I found Jacko had come back without you. The common can be treacherous in parts,' she added, shaking her head gravely.

Treacherous, plus bloody dangerous and unexpectedly disturbing, Alanna supplied silently as she sat down, still with a certain care.

'So, how did you like Dolly?' Mrs Harrington went on. 'A bit quiet now, I dare say, bless her. But come out with me tomorrow, and I'll put you on Caradoc.

'My brother-in-law in Ireland bought him as a stallion, but he nearly wrecked the horse box, kicked out his stall and attacked his girl groom, as well as fighting with the other horses, so Patrick had him gelded and offered him to me as a point to pointer for Gerard.

'But he was still a wild one, and I'd just decided to sell him on when Gerard's cousin took a fancy to him. Came down here at weekends to work with him until Caradoc would come when he whistled.

'Turned him into a lovely smooth ride with the manners of a saint, would you believe? But then,' she added, shrugging, 'gypsies always seem to have a way with horses. It's in their genes, I dare say.'

It was the overt contempt in her voice that told Alanna that it was Zandor's own grandmother who would never intend 'gypsy' to be a compliment—or even a joke. And how vile was that?

Mrs Harrington sent Alanna another bright smile. 'So we'll go out in the morning and see what you make of the darling boy.'

The smile was transferred seamlessly to the housekeeper, entering with a tray. 'Set the coffee down here, Mrs Jackson dear, and we'll serve ourselves.'

She picked up the heavy silver pot. 'I'd guess cream but no sugar. Am I right?'

Alanna, whose mind's eye had been suddenly filled with a sunlit image of a man riding a powerful bay as if they were fused into one, like some ancient Greek centaur, dragged herself back to reality with a start. 'Actually, I take it black.'

Mrs Harrington tutted. 'Ah, now, too much caffeine is bad for the system, so I'm told.'

'I've heard the same thing,' Alanna agreed, taking the cup her hostess handed her. 'But I still prefer it that way.'

She hesitated. 'And tomorrow we'll be going back to London right after breakfast, so, sadly, I'll have to miss out on another ride. But thank you for asking me.' And produced a smile of her own. 'Next time perhaps.'

'Well, there's always that,' Mrs Harrington agreed tranquilly. 'However, I'm afraid, my dear, that I have to disappoint you. Gerard, being the heir, has a number of responsibilities down here at Whitestone, especially now I'm not as young as I was, and we have tenants who'll be wanting to see him tomorrow.'

She nodded. 'I imagine that could take up most of the day, and then we'll need to discuss everything, so he may well be spending the night. And I'm sure you need to get back to your busy life and your career in the big city.'

She sighed. 'Ah, girls today have the best of it. Great jobs and their independence. My own family took it for granted I'd stay at home until I was married, and that's what I did until the blessed day when Gerard's grandfather came to claim me.

'It will be so different for you, dear girl. You can enjoy your freedom.'

She paused, then went on more briskly, 'But my Diana and her husband are leaving before lunch, so I'm sure they'll be glad to give you a lift. I'll ask them, shall I? Or you could speak to Joanne. I've noticed the pair of you hitting it off.'

I bet you have, thought Alanna, sipping her coffee with a fair assumption of composure. So that's how it's done. Nothing as crude as 'Never darken my doors again.'

Just the subtle dagger between the ribs. And if I cared, I'd now be bleeding all over this Persian rug.

As it is, what's twisting the knife is having to accept that Zandor was right. But at least I'll never have to say so. Or not to him, anyway.

Knowing I'll definitely never have to meet him again is actually one of the few advantages of the situation.

However, if Mrs H. thinks I'm going to leave in a huff right here and now, she'll be disappointed. I intend to stick to my guns and depart with dignity.

Aloud, she said calmly, 'Please don't trouble yourself, Mrs Harrington. I can make my own arrangements.'

Or Gerard certainly can, she decided, stonily. I think he owes me that. Because I'm not going round begging for a lift as if I'm a Victorian servant turned off without a character.

Besides, he must know his grandmother's plans for his future, so what on earth prompted him to invite me in the first place?

Therefore, I'm going to have some advice for him too. Grow a backbone before it's too late.

Then, swiftly reverting to the theme of dignified departure, she smilingly accepted another 'absolutely delicious' cup of coffee.

Which proved to be a mistake.

'I believe your father is a lawyer,' Niamh Harrington remarked as she handed back Alanna's cup. 'One of the great professions, I always think. My cousin's son is Dermot Connor-Smith, QC who's made a great name for himself at the criminal bar. I expect your father knows him well.'

'I doubt they've ever met,' Alanna returned composedly after another fortifying sip. 'My father isn't a barrister, and he doesn't work in London.'

'Not in London?' Mrs Harrington's brows rose. 'Isn't that a strange choice?'

'Not at all. He's a partner specialising in probate and family law at a firm based in a small market town called Silworth.' Alanna paused. 'Perhaps you've heard of it?'

Mrs Harrington appeared to consider. 'It doesn't spring to mind. And he finds enough to occupy him there?'

Alanna smiled. 'Oh, yes. He's always busy.'

'And your mother. Does she also have a job?'

'She does part-time work in a charity shop for the homeless, but she's also very involved with the local Women's Institute, and both she and Dad are keen gardeners.'

And so the inquisition continued, demonstrating to Alanna with needle-sharp accuracy just how provincial her background would seem to the Harringtons of Whitestone Abbey.

By the time the meeting drew to its close and she

was graciously released—'I think some of the others are playing croquet on the lawn, my dear. I'm sure you'd be most welcome to join them…'—Alanna's blood was close to boiling.

Whatever she'd resolved privately, it was still not pleasant to be dismissed in such a cavalier fashion. Treated as if she didn't matter, she thought as she stormed upstairs. As if, God help her, she'd somehow been tried and found wanting.

As for croquet, she thought savagely, watch out, world, and Niamh Harrington in particular, if she got her hands on a mallet any time soon.

She flung open the door of her room and marched in, stopping herself just in time from slamming it behind her in case the sound echoed as far as the library and told Gerard's grandmother that her knife had found its target.

Nor did she intend to permit herself to cry, although she knew tears were not far from the surface. She would not, she decided, grant Niamh Harrington that much of a victory either.

She stalked furiously into the bathroom and began to run water into the tub, adding a generous capful of gardenia bath oil, before stripping off her clothes and fastening her hair into a loose knot on top of her head with a small silver comb.

She slid down into the water, closing her eyes and resting her head against the small towelling pillow attached to the back of the bath, feeling the heat permeate through every inch of her chilled and shaking body. Relaxing gradually as she inhaled the fragrance of the gardenia and began to breathe softly and evenly again.

And there she remained, adding more hot water when necessary until she'd recovered a measure of calm, even managing to smile again as she thought what she'd have to tell Susie—strictly edited, naturally. Zandor Varga, if she mentioned him at all, would feature only as Gerard's arrogant boss. Their previous acquaintance would still stay strictly taboo.

And one day, sooner rather than later, she would be able to erase his memory from her life altogether.

As the water drained, she dried herself slowly with one of the soft, fluffy bath towels provided, moisturised her skin with her Azalea body lotion, then wrapping herself, sarong-style, in another towel, she sauntered back into her bedroom, removing her comb and letting her hair tumble round her bare shoulders as she went.

'Ah,' Zandor said softly. 'So there you are.'

He was standing by the bedroom door, leaning a casual shoulder against its frame.

Alanna started violently, dropping the comb and clutching at the towel, which had begun to slip.

She said hoarsely, '*You.* How dare you come in here? Get out at once.'

'It didn't require any particular daring.' He shrugged. 'I came to return some lost property.'

He pointed to the bed and, turning, Alanna saw the sweater she'd dropped in that headlong dash across the common draped neatly across the pillow.

Damnation, she thought, and lifted her chin. 'Then you should have knocked.'

'I did. You didn't seem to be here. And the door was not locked.' He paused. 'Unlike last night.'

So it was you. She managed just in time to choke back the words.

Oh, God, she thought. Why didn't I think of it this morning?

'And you don't need to thank me.' He allowed his gaze to travel over her slowly and appreciatively. 'I am already sufficiently rewarded, believe me.'

She felt her skin warm. 'In that case, kindly leave.' She spoke crisply. 'I'd like to get dressed.'

'Then do so,' he drawled. 'After all, watching you put your clothes back on again is one of the few things I haven't yet enjoyed in your company.'

The breath caught in her throat. She said unevenly, 'If you don't get out now, I'll scream the house down.'

His brows lifted mockingly. 'Rather extreme action to take with someone you supposedly met only twenty-four hours ago,' he commented. 'How would you explain it?'

'I wouldn't have to,' she said defiantly. 'Your reputation with women apparently speaks for itself.'

'No,' he said softly. 'But gossip certainly does. My Cousin Joanne has been busy.'

She said huskily, 'Or perhaps she speaks from bitter experience.'

'No.' His tone was harsh. 'She does not.' He paused. 'I admit I considered it at one time, but then I remembered I used to be fond of her.'

Alanna drew a ragged breath. 'Whereas with me you didn't even have that excuse.'

'No,' he said. 'With you, my lovely one, I had no excuse at all. None.'

He straightened. Came away from the door.

Alanna shrank. 'Keep your distance. Don't dare to lay a hand on me.'

'Now you are being absurd.' He glanced at his watch. 'It is barely an hour until lunch.' He sent her a crooked smile. 'Certainly not time for anything I might have in mind. As you may remember.'

'You,' she said unevenly, 'can go to hell.'

He opened the door. Looked back at her. He said quietly, '"*Why, this is hell, nor am I out of it.*" I am sure you recognise the quotation.'

And went, closing the door behind him.

For a long moment, Alanna remained exactly where she was, staring at the solid wooden panels. Then she stumbled across the room and—belatedly—turned the key in the lock once again.

Better safe than sorry, she thought, and knew just how ridiculous that was. Because she certainly wouldn't be safe until she left the abbey behind her for ever. And it was equally certain, she told herself, that her meeting with Zandor Varga was something she'd regret for the rest of her life.

It was almost time for the midday buffet on the terrace that Gerard had mentioned on the journey down when she eventually went downstairs, casually dressed in a brief khaki cotton skirt and a cream short-sleeved top, her hair brushed back and confined at the nape of her neck with a tortoiseshell clasp.

She had scrutinised herself closely before leaving her room, and was reassured there was nothing in her appearance to suggest she'd spent the last few hours on an emotional roller coaster.

So, outwardly, she was together, and if, inwardly, her composure seemed to be hanging by a thread, that was something else to add to her list of little secrets.

To her surprise, she found Gerard waiting at the foot of the stairs.

He said, 'I was just coming to find you.'

She shrugged coolly. 'Whereas I wouldn't have known where to start looking for you.' She allowed that to sink in before glancing at her watch. 'Am I late? Due for an entry in your Aunt Caroline's bad books?'

'No, not at all.' He paused. 'In fact, I thought

we'd give the buffet a miss and drive over to the village. The pub does a pretty good ploughman's, but there are other places further on in Aldchester if you'd prefer.' He hesitated again. 'Or we can stay here.'

He seemed to be making a real effort, so Alanna relented and gave him a smile. 'A ploughman's and some cider would be terrific.'

He grinned back. 'And it's perfect weather for a convertible, so why don't I get Zan to loan me his Lamborghini for the afternoon.'

'No!' She saw immediately that her instinctive negative had been too quick and far too emphatic. 'I mean—as you say, it's a lovely day and he may want to use it himself. Besides, I really like the Mercedes.'

'Well, there's no accounting for tastes,' he said cheerfully. 'But it's your decision, so let's go.'

The pub in Whitestone village was called The Abbot's Retreat.

'He can't have been a very saintly abbot,' Alanna commented, as they parked the car and walked round to the gardens at the rear. 'Not if he had to retreat to a pub.'

Gerard grinned. 'Don't condemn the poor guy too quickly. Tradition says that there was once a hermitage on this site, somewhere the monks came for solitude and prayer. And traces of a much earlier building have actually been found in the cellars.'

'We'll give him the benefit of the doubt,' Alanna decided as they found a table beside a stream overhung with willows. 'And I wouldn't blame him either way.'

The ploughman's lunches were substantial, with slices of home-cured ham alongside the mature cheese, salad and fresh crusty bread.

To her own surprise, Alanna ate every scrap.

'Great idea,' she said as she finished her cider, and put down her empty glass. 'Congratulations.'

'I felt something was needed,' Gerard admitted ruefully. 'The weekend so far isn't exactly proceeding as I planned. I seem to be at other people's beck and call the whole time. But that's going to stop.'

He smiled with faint awkwardness. 'From here on, it's you and me against the world.'

Alanna felt a stirring of alarm.

She said steadily, 'I'm not sure what you mean.'

He reached across and took her hand. 'Alanna—I know it's too soon, but I want you to agree to become engaged to me.'

Her lips parted in a gasp of sheer astonishment. She said faintly, 'But we hardly know each other…'

'If you're saying we've never been on intimate terms, that's quite true.' He hesitated. 'Alanna, I was in a bad place when you quite literally fell into my life. And as I got to know you, I had the impression that you'd been in a similar situation.

'I—I've never asked you about it, or talked about

my own problems because I'd come to see that nothing can be gained by endlessly rehashing past mistakes.'

She swallowed. 'Well, we can certainly agree about that,' she said unevenly. 'But, Gerard…'

'Please hear me out.' His fingers tightened round hers. 'Right now, I'm simply offering an engagement, not pressuring you into marriage—or anything else for that matter. I think—I hope we could be happy together, if we gave each other the chance.'

She gave him a straight look. 'But there are other people who might not be happy at all.'

'You mean Grandam.' His mouth tightened. 'I love her dearly, Alanna, but she has to realise she can't control my life. Not any more.'

Alanna wasn't too sure of that, just as she was totally certain this engagement idea was a path she didn't want to follow. Because marriage was out of the question.

Even if she'd fallen in love with him, twenty-four hours at the abbey would have warned her to think again and run for her life. For all kinds of reasons.

But to tell him so bluntly would be unkind.

A bad place. Well, as he'd guessed, she knew all about that. And that was another good reason for letting him down lightly.

She said quietly, 'This has come as such a total surprise. You have to give me some time. Let me think about it.'

'Take as long as you need. And as I said, I won't try to change our relationship—push you into something you're not ready for. So let's just see how it goes. Shall we?'

'Yes,' she said. 'I suppose.' She hesitated. 'But, Gerard, I'm not promising anything. I can't. Not yet.'

Not ever...

She added, 'You must understand that.'

She felt dazed as they returned to the car. If he'd stripped naked and jumped into the stream, she couldn't have been more astonished, although she supposed it explained the unusually proprietorial attitude he'd shown since the start of the weekend.

Which must have also set Niamh Harrington's alarm bells ringing.

Well, let her worry, she thought with grim determination. At the party tonight, for the first and last time, she'll be seeing me in full devoted girlfriend mode. And to hell with the consequences.

CHAPTER SIX

'THAT,' SAID JOANNE REVERENTLY, 'is one gorgeous dress.'

Alanna smiled at her. 'Glad you like it.'

She had to admit the soft colour glimmered even in the fading light from her window, and it did indeed cling in all the right places.

She remembered thinking when she bought it that the weekend could be a turning point for her. And how right she'd been—even if it wasn't exactly as anticipated. More twists than a corkscrew, she thought with an inward grimace before adding lightly, 'I want to make Gerard proud of me tonight.'

'I should think he'll burst with it.' Joanne giggled naughtily. 'And the Hon. Felicity will burst too— for a different reason.'

'Felicity?' Alanna queried. 'Oh, the girl your grandmother suggested should go riding with me.'

'That's the one.' Joanne nodded. 'Lord Bradham's only child—and therefore loaded. Not to say spoiled.' She rolled her eyes. 'She and Gerard had a boy-girl thing for a little while in their teens, and Grandam periodically tries to revive it. Fat chance, on his side at least, so you don't have to worry.'

'I couldn't be less worried if I tried,' Alanna assured her. Although not for the reason you think, she added silently.

'Besides Dad has always said that if Grandam got her way, she could live to regret it,' Joanne went on. 'You see, Felicity runs this very upmarket letting agency for wealthy visitors from abroad.'

She grinned. 'He reckons that as soon as the ink on the marriage certificate was dry, she'd have Grandam whistled out of here into a purpose-built annexe at the manor with a live-in carer, while she rented out the abbey for megabucks to some foreign oligarch.'

Alanna smiled too, but felt a touch of compunction.

'I can't imagine Gerard allowing that to happen.'

'That,' said Joanne darkly, 'is because you haven't met Felicity.'

She looked at her watch. 'We'd better go down. People will be arriving soon, and Grandam likes the whole family assembled to greet them.'

Which hardly includes me, thought Alanna. But this is the one and only time so I won't argue.

Gerard was waiting in the hall below. He looked them both over and said, 'Wow,' before offering them each an arm and escorting them ceremoniously into the drawing room.

'Ah,' said Niamh Harrington. 'So here are the latecomers at last.' She beamed at them. 'But it's been worth the wait.'

'Not,' Alanna murmured inwardly, catching the steely glint in the cherubic blue eyes. Nor did she miss the imperious gesture summoning Gerard to his grandmother's side or the low-voiced altercation that followed.

However, the Dennisons were smiling and waving, so she prudently got out of the firing line and went to join them with Joanne, just as the first guests started arriving.

The room was soon full, the extra staff hired for the occasion circulating busily with trays of drinks and canapés. And because the invitees were all local people and already acquainted, the talk and laughter levels rose accordingly.

Alanna, her hand beginning to ache through being vigorously shaken, and her head reeling with names she knew she would never remember, was thankful this was a one-off event and soon to be forgotten.

Although some moments might linger, unwanted, in her memory, like glancing up and seeing Zandor, watching her through the crowd, and raising his glass in a mocking salute.

She turned away abruptly nearly bumping into a tall girl, stick-insect-thin in a pale blue dress, her glossy chestnut hair woven into an ornate coronet on top of her head.

'Oh, hi.' Her voice was a high-pitched drawl, her accent cut glass. 'I haven't seen you before,' she went on, looking Alanna up and down. 'I suppose you're a friend of Joanne, who seems to have vanished, so tell her, will you, that I'm still waiting to hear from that journo chap of hers. It's been weeks, so not impressed. Not impressed at all.'

And with a nod, she walked on.

'And that,' said Joanne appearing from nowhere. 'Is dear Felicity.'

Alanna stared at her then began to smile. 'Were you hiding?'

Joanne grinned back. 'I'll say. Ducked down behind the sofa when I saw her coming. She's apparently campaigning to be nominated Businesswoman of the Decade or something and when she heard I was dating someone from the *Chronicle* she started pestering me to get him to interview her about her amazing success. Another glass ceiling smashed, etc.

'Chris's response was that all advertising has to be paid for, but I don't relish having to tell her so.'

Alanna nodded. 'We have the same problem promoting authors. There has to be a story apart from the one they've written.'

'Whereas Felicity's story comprises one word— "Me",' Joanne said gloomily. 'I can hardly tell her that either.'

'No,' Alanna agreed. 'But how about saying he's now considering doing a composite piece featuring all the candidates for the award. Equal publicity for all.'

'Making her just one of a crowd. That will go down like a lead balloon.' Joanne gave a sigh of relief. 'Alanna, I can see you're going to be a real asset to this family.'

Only for a few hours more, Alanna thought, crossing her fingers behind her back.

She'd expected Gerard to return and join her at some point, but seeing him standing, stony-faced behind his grandmother's sofa, soon convinced her that this was not going to happen. A view substantially reinforced when the places flanking Mrs Harrington became occupied by Felicity Bradham and a tall grey-haired man that Alanna guessed was her father.

The party reached a climax when a large birthday cake was wheeled in on a trolley, and ceremoniously cut by Niamh Harrington so that slices could be distributed to the departing guests.

In its wake came an enormous basket of flowers—'Paid for by all the locals, including the tenants,' Joanne whispered. 'Feudal or what!'—and presented by Lord Bradham, who then led the company in singing, 'For she's a jolly good fellow'.

Despite all evidence to the contrary, Alanna said silently, reminding herself, as people began to leave, there was now only the family dinner to endure.

As she'd expected, she was seated once again

about as far from Gerard as it was possible to get, and if she'd been falling in love with him, that would have rankled.

But, under the circumstances, it was probably no bad thing, she thought, noting with amusement that Felicity had been seated next to him.

Besides, her placement meant that she was in the same congenial company as the previous evening, which delighted her, and away from Mrs Harrington's watchful gaze, which pleased her even more.

Now all she had to do was try to appear oblivious to the presence of Zandor who was seated between Caroline Healey and Gerard's mother on the opposite side of the table, but not, thankfully, in her direct eyeline.

The meal began with chilled avocado soup, continued with poached salmon mayonnaise, followed by duck in a rich cherry sauce, and completed with individual vanilla and honeycomb cheesecakes.

Gerard had explained that after the dessert there would be a pause before coffee was served, so that a birthday toast could be drunk before his grandmother opened the gifts waiting on a side table, Alanna's photograph frame among them.

An offering that would almost certainly find its way to a charity shop in the near future, she thought with a mental shrug.

An expectant silence fell as Gerard rose to his

feet, glass in hand. He spoke briefly and affection-ately about his grandmother then proposed the toast to her health adding, 'And, of course, many happy returns of the day.' Words that were echoed round the table as everyone rose to drink before singing a chorus of 'Happy birthday to you'.

After which they all resumed their seats but with one exception.

Gerard, still standing, cleared his throat and smiled round the table.

'Now I have another toast to propose. And, I hope, another happy surprise for Grandam's birth-day.'

He paused. 'Earlier today, Alanna and I became engaged. And I would like you all to welcome my fiancée to the family and drink to our future hap-piness.'

The shock wave that ran through the room was almost tangible, and if anyone else had been in-volved, Alanna might even have found it amusing.

As it was, she had a curious sensation that she'd been turned to stone.

She wanted to leap to her feet, shouting, 'No, it's not true. I never agreed to it. I never would.'

But she seemed to be pinned, silent, to her chair.

Nor was she the only one. Niamh Harrington was rigid, her fresh colour fading to reveal two harsh spots of blusher.

While across the table…

In spite of herself, Alanna found she was looking at Zandor, her nerve-ends tingling as she saw the harsh line of his mouth, and met the stark brilliance of his gaze which went beyond shock to anger and something terribly, unbearably like pity, mingled with contempt.

And saw too the faint shake of his head, as if emphasising silently his earlier warning: 'It's never going to happen.'

A challenge issued and accepted as Alanna felt rage and resentment take swift and uncontrollable possession of her.

How dared he look at her like that? she thought as she got to her feet. What damned right had he—or anyone else in that room—to judge her? Or ordain her future?

Well, to hell with the lot of them.

She walked, forcing herself to seem quietly, happily self-possessed, to where Gerard stood, and slipped her hand through his arm.

'Darling,' she said softly. 'How naughty of you. I thought we were going wait—to keep it our little secret for a while.' And lifted her smiling face for him to kiss her on the mouth.

In the next instant, the ongoing silence was broken by Maurice Dennison, rising from his chair.

'Congratulations, my boy, and every good wish to you, my dear,' he said heartily. 'We couldn't be more happy for you both—could we, everyone?'

And as he glanced round the table, the others stood in turn, murmuring 'To Gerard and Alanna' as they drank. With Zandor, the last one of all, merely raising his glass in a negligently token gesture.

Which Alanna knew was intended to fool no one—least of all herself.

'I can't believe you did that.' An hour later, a stormy Alanna faced Gerard on the terrace under the guise of a romantic moonlight stroll. 'I thought we had an agreement.'

'We still do,' he said urgently. 'I swear that hasn't changed.' He spread his hands. 'But you've no idea of the pressure I've been under.'

'Actually,' she said, 'I think I have. But I've allowed my inbuilt aversion to being used to take precedence on this occasion.'

'Well, thank you, anyway, for going along with it.'

'As opposed to calling you a liar in front of your family?' She sighed. 'Oh, Gerard, what a mess.'

He said with faint stiffness, 'It doesn't have to be. My suggestion we should become engaged, even on a trial basis, was perfectly sincere. And that's what's going to happen. We have to give ourselves a chance.'

'Not easy with half your relations asking if we've set the date yet, and the others behaving as if you've had a mental breakdown,' she said bitterly.

Except I'm the crazy one for agreeing to this engagement fiasco when I know I haven't the slightest intention of marrying you.

Aloud, she added, 'And as I'd rather not face them again, will you take me round to the side door, please, so I can go straight up to my room.'

'Yes, if that's what you want.' He paused. 'But they may find it strange.'

'In which case,' Alanna said coolly, 'it will fit in nicely with the rest of the evening's events.'

Alone in her bedroom, with the door safely locked, she took off her dress and hung it carefully away, then put on her robe and lay down on top of the bed, staring into space as she recapped everything that had happened.

After Gerard's announcement, the opening of Niamh's presents, which followed, seemed a total anticlimax.

She certainly exclaimed and enthused, but it was clear her heart wasn't in it. When she unwrapped Alanna's photograph frame, she studied it in silence for a moment, then looked up, smiling.

'How thoughtful,' she said softly. 'I shall keep it for a picture of your wedding, dear girl.'

If, of course, you can find one small enough, Alanna supplied silently as she smiled back.

When they returned to the drawing room for coffee, Joanne flew across the room and threw her arms round first Alanna then Gerard, hugging them both exuberantly.

'Well, you kept that up your sleeves,' she teased, adding more quietly, 'By the way, Felicity and her father have made their excuses and gone home. Grandam won't be too pleased about that, but Zandor's leaving as well which should make up for it.'

Gerard gave her an affectionate squeeze. 'Jo, you're the limit.'

'That's saying something in this company,' she threw back, before flitting off as light and graceful as a dragonfly, while Alanna was left with a sudden image of Zandor, heading off alone in his Lamborghini, and told herself that, at least, she had something to be thankful for.

Yet, to her own chagrin, found herself asking Gerard, 'Was your cousin not expected to leave tonight?'

'Oh, he comes and goes as he pleases.' Gerard shrugged. 'Always has, always will.' He gave a faint snort. 'He hasn't even got a permanent base in London, just uses the penthouse suite in a hotel, which probably belongs to him anyway. He's probably rushed off because he has some big deal brewing somewhere.'

He paused. 'His father and grandfather may well have been dodgy customers, but, my God, they were successful, and he is too. He has heavy media interests as well as the tourist industry, and he owns the Alphamaro restaurant chain. Bazaar Vert is just a small part of his empire.'

'I see,' said Alanna, who didn't.

She had no time to consider this unsettling information because, after that, everyone else had something to say to them, with differing degrees of cordiality, of which the most telling was Meg Harrington's cool, 'I wish you luck.'

She didn't need to add, 'You'll need it,' because it was right there in her tone.

And Alanna responded, 'Thank you so much,' with a smile so firmly nailed on it made her face ache.

In fact, now she was back and thankfully alone, she seemed to be aching all over, inwardly as well as out, and knew that if this had been a genuine engagement she'd have been shedding despondent tears by now.

As it was, she reviewed the exchange she'd had with Gerard earlier as they walked round to the side door.

'If your grandmother's so picky about your future wife, I'm surprised she hasn't paired you with Joanne,' she'd commented. 'She appears very fond of her.'

'She is.' He shrugged. 'But even if Jo and I fancied each other—which we don't—it would make no difference. We'd still be first cousins.'

'But what difference does that make?' Alanna frowned. 'Cousins marrying isn't against English law.'

'However it's very definitely against Grandam's law, which is all that matters round here,' he returned flatly. 'She has these rigid rules about blood lines and good breeding stock, which make the Medes and the Persians look like beginners.'

She said slowly, 'Actually Joanne mentioned something of the sort, but I thought she was joking.'

'Oh, no.' There was an odd bitterness in his voice. 'It's all deadly serious, believe me. Expect some hefty questions about your family and forbears one of these days. She likes to go back several generations.'

'Does she really?' Alanna said tartly. 'And people put up with that, do they?'

'Usually,' said Gerard equally shortly, and there the matter rested.

Not that it will ever apply to me, Alanna thought, frowning at the memory. Except as a reminder why I'd never—ever—fit into the Harrington clan.

Tomorrow, on the way back, she and Gerard would have to concoct some excellent reasons why there should be no notice in the papers, or, heaven help her, some gruesome family engagement party with her astonished parents who were only marginally aware of Gerard's existence and had certainly never met him.

Although that would probably have to change, she thought reluctantly.

She supposed she could use pressure of work—plus the ongoing uncertainty over Hawkseye's future—as an excuse for postponing any formal announcement, even though she couldn't imagine it carrying much weight.

She was pretty sure that the future Mrs Gerard Harrington would not be expected to pursue a career. She'd be far too busy producing a brood of beautifully un-spavined children with antecedents stretching back to William the Conqueror.

'And good luck to her,' she muttered under her breath.

But what on earth, she wondered as she undressed and brushed her hair, was she going to tell Susie who, in about twelve hours' time, would be waiting to hear about the weekend in all its grisly detail? And who at the same time would be meeting Gerard?

After all, she could hardly let him drive her home without inviting him in, even with all those cats just waiting to leap out of the bag.

She'd sworn to herself that she'd keep no more secrets from Susie and meant it, yet knew all she could do was tighten the bag more securely and hope it would never need to be opened.

Unless, of course, she called the whole thing off,

telling Gerard that a night's rest had made her re-think the situation and decide it was impossible.

Except that would be seen as a victory by Niamh Harrington—and also by that other grandson who was now back in her own life—like an unexploded grenade threatening to destroy her hard-won and carefully constructed tranquillity.

And simply muttering 'To hell with him' at intervals wasn't working.

"'Why, this is hell, nor am I out of it...'"

Suddenly she recalled where she'd heard those words before—at a university performance of Marlowe's *Doctor Faustus*—and how a shiver had gone down her spine as the demon tempter Mephistopheles uttered his anguished lament over his banishment from heaven.

Since then, she'd succumbed to another brand of temptation, she thought, biting her lip, and the paradise she'd lost was her peace of mind.

And while she maintained even a tenuous connection with the Harrington family, that was how it would stay.

But she'd made her choice and she'd stick to it somehow, she told herself as she got into bed. After all, it wouldn't be for ever, and maybe Zandor's sudden departure was a good sign. An admission of defeat, indicating their paths would not cross again.

I can but hope, she thought, and resolutely closed her eyes.

But she soon found that all the positive thinking in the world couldn't bring the longed-for oblivion of sleep.

Because Gerard's casual reference to Zandor's living arrangements had re-ignited all her memories of the night they'd spent together and now, in spite of herself, they were still there, burning in her mind.

She realised she could recite almost every detail about the penthouse suite—the individual jewel colours of the cushions in the ivory sitting room—the embossed star pattern on the magnificent purple quilt—probably even the thread count in the expensive snowy bedlinen.

Total recall, and if only it could be confined to the décor, not a problem.

As it was…

She turned restlessly, seeking for a cool place on the pillow, pushing away the sheet at one moment because it was strangling her and dragging it round her the next, as if she needed its protection.

I left, she thought desperately. I did the right thing—the only thing—and walked away. And he—he let me go.

So how, in spite of that, did it all go so terribly wrong?

Well, she could no longer use the champagne as an excuse, because, if she was honest—and maybe it was time she was—she'd drunk far more at various uni parties and managed to emerge unscathed.

So, why had this time been so different?

Someone once said to understand all was to forgive all, and perhaps that was exactly what she needed to do if she was ever to mend her shattered self-respect.

Instead she'd preferred to believe that Zandor was simply a dangerous predator that she'd been too inexperienced to evade.

Had clung to that conviction ever since. Even embellished it.

Yet all she'd had to do was walk into the lift, and her failure to do this did not automatically transform her into a victim. Or him into a villain...

I was reaching to press the button, she thought, but then I—looked back. And everything changed.

Because he was just—standing there, silent and still in the doorway, watching her go, and she knew suddenly that she'd never seen anyone look so totally alone.

And she was turning, running back along the thick carpet, even stumbling a little, so that when she flung herself at him, his arms were waiting to catch her and lift her off her feet, high into his embrace, his mouth locking fiercely to hers as he carried her back into the suite, kicking the door shut behind them.

Arms fastened round his neck, she gave herself

up to the moment, exchanging kiss for kiss as Zandor strode with her to the adjoining room and the waiting bed.

He placed her carefully in its centre and lay beside her, kissing her again deeply and unhurriedly, his hands recommencing their exploration of her slender body, making her skin stir and her nerve-endings quiver in shy delight even through the barriers of her clothing.

So that when, this time, he drew down her zip and removed her dress completely, her little sigh was one of acceptance, not protest, knowing that she wanted—needed—the tenderness of his touch on her naked flesh.

And saw him smile into her eyes, telling her silently that her need was not only recognised but shared.

His fingertips were like gossamer as they strayed over the curve of her face and travelled down her throat to stroke her bared shoulders and the soft vulnerability of her underarms before tracing a slow path across the delicate mounds of her breasts where they swelled above the lacy confinement of her bra.

Alanna sighed again, head thrown back, her spine arching under the irresistible response of her senses to this subtle web he was so skilfully weaving around them, first with his hands and now even more devastatingly with his lips.

She was hardly aware of the moment when he removed her bra, only of the exquisite instant when his mouth closed on one naked breast, suckling it gently while his tongue flickered across her rapidly hardening nipple, offering a pleasure that was almost pain.

Awakening inside her for the first time the deep, hot ache of desire. And the inevitable demand for it to be satisfied.

And now, lying alone in the darkness, she heard herself say aloud, her voice ragged, 'I never knew. Oh, God, until that moment I never realised…'

CHAPTER SEVEN

PERHAPS THAT WAS the explanation, she thought, as well as her only viable excuse. That she'd suddenly heard the ticking of a different kind of biological clock telling her it was time to leave the armour-plated innocence of girlhood behind her and become a woman at last.

And Zan had been there—available—the wrong man at, questionably, the right time. And they'd used each other.

Nothing more. Nothing less.

Except…

She pressed her clenched fist to her lips as she remembered cradling his head between her hands, stroking the dark silk of his hair as she held him against her excited breasts, unable to control her soft moans of bewildered delight as he pleasured them.

Would she have been the same with any man? she wondered with faint shame. Wasn't it that fear that had made her cling so fiercely to celibacy ever since? Maybe that was the best—the safest thing to believe.

Because anything else was totally impossible.

She closed her eyes so tightly that tiny lights danced behind her lids, telling herself she'd remembered enough. Too much…

Although there seemed to be no peace for her yet.

'Do you know how beautiful you are?' His voice was there in her head, restrained, husky, and somehow inescapable.

His face imprinted on her mind—his expression serious—intent as he looked down at her.

She never considered herself a beauty but in that moment, in his arms, she'd almost believed it could be true.

Even now she seemed to feel his touch curling across her skin, making her burn and shiver, reminding her all too potently of how his hands had slid down to her hips, ridding her of the few inches of lace which still covered her.

When, for a moment, her earlier shyness returned, as much for being naked in front of a man for the first time, as for the prospect of what was to come.

The moment when she would give up her innocence for ever.

Zandor kissed her again, his tongue moving slowly, sweetly against hers, while his fingers stroked her slender thighs coaxing them to part for him.

With a tiny sob she yielded, offering him every last secret her body had to give.

And his response was equally generous, his hands gentle and exquisitely precise as he started to explore her silken heat. To guide her with infinite care and tenderness into the dark labyrinth of total arousal.

Sensation uncurled inside her like a slow flame and her breathing quickened as she felt the tiny bud hidden between the soft damp petals of her labia swelling into aching excitement under the skilful play of his fingers.

As she realised that the control she'd always taken for granted was irretrievably slipping away, and this scared her because it was happening too soon and much too fast.

She wanted to ask him to pause, at least momentarily, so that she could regain some command of the rational being who'd existed in her skin when the evening began. So that she could think.

But the planned words failed her, emerging instead as a little broken moan, more pleading than protest.

Warning her that it was already too late. That she was already lost—overtaken—consumed by the incredible intensity of the hunger he was creating with such frightening ease.

By the astonishing delicacy of his touch as his fingers moved, penetrating slowly but very surely, the scalding heat of her awakened womanhood, making her gasp and writhe in helpless longing against his hand.

He kissed her parted lips, his tongue flickering against hers, as he returned to her tiny tumescent mound, caressing it into a new agony as delicious as it was fierce.

Alanna found herself focussing almost blindly on her body's reactions to his caresses. At the astounding, even frightening sense that every atom of her being was slowly but inexorably tightening like a clenched fist. Drawn into an upward spiral in response to his touch.

And that a voice which, to her shame, she hardly recognised as her own, was begging—whimpering—for release from this—oh, God—this almost intolerable but wholly exquisite pressure that Zandor was inflicting on her.

Then, as a final raw sob was torn from her straining throat, he said her name and his hand moved compellingly, insistently, snapping the thread that was holding her in this frantic torment, and sending her tumbling, her body throbbing, ravaged by a pleasure that bordered on violence, into some deep and shimmering void.

Where, the ecstatic spasms slowly quietening into peace, she lay at last, lost for words, but looking up at him through a blur of tears.

'Ah, no.' Zandor's voice was very tender as he drew her close, pillowing her head on his chest. 'Don't cry, my darling. My own sweet.'

But these, she thought, were happy tears…

Aloud, she said huskily, 'You see—I—I didn't know…'

'You think you have to tell me that?' He kissed the top of her head.

No, she thought, with a sudden, startling despondency. He knows far too much already. Not just about me, but women in general. But it's too late to worry about that now. Especially as I have no one but myself to blame.

If blame was the apposite word when she was lying in his arms, her body—her entire being—replete and purring with unforgettable delight.

And still with so much else to learn...

The thought came from nowhere, and refused to be dismissed. It clung there in the corner of her mind like a whispered promise. Intriguing. Irresistible.

And she did not even try to resist. Instead she moved even closer, stretching slowly, languorously against the entire length of his body, to be reminded by the brush of fabric on her skin that he was still fully dressed.

Total self-absorption or what, she asked herself, aware that her reaction to the discovery was more sensual than amused. Leading her to the conclusion that this was a situation overdue for a remedy.

She raised a hand and began slowly to unfasten the remaining buttons on his shirt, only for his fingers to close on hers, halting her as she started to ease the garment from his shoulders.

He said softly, 'This is unwise. I think it would be better—safer—for us to get some sleep.'

She touched smiling lips to the smooth bronze of his bared chest, inhaling, as she did so, the intoxicating scent of his skin, warm and clean with a hint of sandalwood.

'But I'm not tired,' she returned. 'And I don't believe you are either.'

She freed her hand, and, all inhibition flown in the still tingling euphoria of her first orgasm, allowed her fingers to trail down to the waistband of his pants, adding, 'Isn't that true?'

'Yes.' The word seemed forced from him. 'But are you truly sure this is what you want?'

She laughed up at him. 'What will it take to convince you?'

'Much too little.' His tone was rueful, and for a moment he seemed about to continue his resistance. Then, with a faint shrug, he sat up, peeling off his shirt and tossing it to the floor beside the bed before unzipping his pants and discarding them too. Finally he stripped off his silk shorts and sent them to join his other clothes.

Naked, he was frankly magnificent and Alanna lay back against the pillows, the breath catching in her throat as she looked at him, wondering dazedly where and how he'd acquired his all-over tan.

He reached for her, drawing her gently back into his arms. Holding her, his cheek against her hair.

He said quietly, 'Wishing now that you'd opted for safety, Alanna?'

She swallowed. 'No. It's just that…' She hesitated, uncertain how to continue, and he nodded.

'You're nervous?' The query was supremely matter-of-fact.

'Well, yes. A little…'

'And so am I,' he admitted. 'You see, this is a first time for me too.'

Alanna stared up at him. 'A first time?' she echoed in disbelief, then blushed. 'Oh—I see.' She hesitated. 'Is it—really a problem?'

'Only because I'm afraid that I may hurt you.' He took her hand and raised it to his lips. 'I can only promise that I will try to be gentle.'

Gentleness, she thought. Was that really what she wanted from him, first time or not? Wasn't some instinct telling her what she really needed was to be a woman with her man? Nothing more, but certainly nothing less…

Her flush deepened. She said constrictedly, 'And I'm just scared I'll be a terrible disappointment.'

He drew her even closer, his firm chest grazing her nipples, the heated power of his arousal nudging gently against her thighs.

'Then why don't we both relax?' he whispered. 'Simply enjoy the moment—and each other?'

And, bending his head, he kissed her parted lips. As the kiss deepened into a sweet, lingering tangle of tongues, Alanna found herself whispering silently, 'Yes—oh, yes…' as her senses stirred again into potent and irresistible desire.

Her hands slid upwards, almost of their own volition, clasping his shoulders, spanning their breadth, discovering with a kind of wonder the strength of bone and play of muscle beneath the smooth skin.

A man's body was hitherto uncharted territory for her, but this first, tentative exploration grew in confidence when she heard his soft intake of breath as her fingers strayed across his shoulder blades, then down the long, supple length of his spine as if she was committing each vertebra to memory.

At the base of his spine, she paused, letting one finger trace tiny, tantalising circles on this sensitive area and heard him groan softly, huskily before she moved down, her hands splaying across his buttocks, her palms smoothing the taut, muscular flesh as his whole body quivered under her caress.

Why had no one told her that simply touching like this—evoking from him this tense, trembling response—could give her a pleasure that was almost raw and a sense of triumph that she'd allowed that unknown sixth sense to take over?

Telling her at the same time that she needed more. So much more. She wanted to be under his skin, absorbed into him—into the entire male mystery of him. To become, somehow, totally, bone of his bone and flesh of his flesh.

Zandor raised his head and looked down at her, the silver eyes clouded, smoky with desire.

He whispered hoarsely, 'Take care, my sweet. I'm not made of iron.'

'No?' There was a smile in her voice. She moved away from him a little, creating a space to allow her hands to glide over his narrow hips then move inward slowly, teasingly, across his flat belly.

She let a fingertip brush him there—*there*—on the rounded velvety tip of him and felt the powerful shaft almost leap into her hand.

'Oh, God.' His voice was almost anguished. 'Alanna—my lovely one—no. You don't know what you're doing to me.'

'Probably not. But if I make a mistake,' she returned softly as her fingers slid slowly downwards, 'I'm sure you'll put me right.'

Her touch was delicate, almost enquiring at first, creating a gentle rhythm all its own, but soon becoming more confident, even adventurous.

Zandor was very still, his eyes closed, the long eyelashes a dark shadow against his skin, his face taut and strained, his entire body tense. All this plus the fluctuations in his breathing told her that he was fighting with near desperation to maintain some element of self-control under her caress.

And she was in no sense immune to his reactions.

Inwardly, she was trembling, her body scalding in its own irresistible need, hovering on the brink of total meltdown.

She whispered 'Zan' on a little sigh that echoed the ache in her flesh as she moved, turning on to her back and spreading herself for him in welcome.

And, as he lifted himself over her, taking him to the liquid yielding heat of her. Feeling him at last where she wanted him—craved him—her body opening for him as he eased his slow, infinitely careful way into her, arms braced on either side of her slenderness, looking down into her face, his gaze alert for any sign of discomfort.

Alanna drew a long, almost victorious breath, then lifted her legs, locking them round his lean hips, silently urging him to go deeper. To possess her utterly.

He said thickly, 'Oh, God, my sweet—my angel,' and responded instantly, thrusting further and further into her with long, smooth strokes, tacitly commanding her to follow his lead with every potent movement, then bending his head so his mouth could once again find hers in the fire of mutual and unrestrained passion.

Her hands went up to his shoulders, gripping them tightly, almost frantically as he filled her completely. As he compelled her onwards with every powerful drive of his loins, their sweat-dampened bodies moving together in a kind of blind unison.

Forcing her to discover the first enticing quivers of anticipation stirring within the hidden reaches of her being.

To recognise these sensations and reach for them, surrendering herself, mind and body, to their growing intensity and their ultimate promise. Joining once more that inescapable, ecstatic spiral as it drew her inexorably upwards.

She heard Zandor breathe, 'Now…' and she was there—at the peak, crying out, then falling—consumed—overwhelmed—by the convulsions of rapture tearing through her body.

Hearing his own fierce groan of release as he buried his face against her throat and let his body shudder into hers.

Afterwards she lay, wrapped closely in his arms, until the final trembling slowly ebbed away and a measure of peace returned.

She wanted to say something, but all she could think of was 'Thank you' which would sound ridiculously childish.

Instead she put up a hand and stroked his face, her fingers tracing a path from one high cheekbone down to his chin.

Zandor captured her hand, biting softly at her fingertips.

'I hope you're not hinting I need to shave,' he whispered. 'Because right now I haven't the strength to make it to the bathroom.'

'No,' she said. 'It's not that.' She hesitated, then added candidly, 'I think I just like touching you.'

'Hang onto that blessed thought.' He paused. 'However, I think we should stop living dangerously and get some sleep. Because tomorrow, my sweet, you and I need to have a serious talk.'

She wanted to protest that she wasn't sleepy, but knew it wasn't true, because a kind of blissful lethargy was already stealing over her, which might also deal with the prospect of sharing a bed for the first time.

So many first times, she thought drowsily as Zandor arranged the pillows and drew the covers over them both. And all of them—wonderful.

She awoke with a start and lay for a moment totally disorientated, staring across at the sliver of pale morning light penetrating the room through a gap in long curtains she did not recognise.

She became aware of a movement in the bed beside her and turned her head slowly and saw Zandor lying with his back to her, his skin burnished against the white linen.

And felt her heart rate lift to panic as memories of the previous night came flooding back. Too vivid. Too all encompassing. Everything she'd done, and, even worse, everything she'd said.

'This isn't happening,' she whispered under her breath. 'It can't be. I must be still asleep and having a bad dream—that's all. Oh, please let that be all...'

But her body's faint soreness had already presented her with a stark reminder that it was all true. That she'd suddenly abandoned her determined defences against the perils of casual sex and given herself to a complete stranger. Lost her virginity to an almost anonymous bird of passage who lived out of a suitcase.

But a man who might also be waking up at any moment. Wanting to have 'a serious talk'. And perhaps more...

Well, she could tell herself that certainly wasn't going to happen, but he might insist, and she wasn't sure she could fight him off—or, if she was honest, that she'd even want to.

She pressed her clenched fist to her mouth to stifle a little moan of shame.

Calm down, she adjured herself fiercely. Forget what you've done—and particularly said—and use whatever's left of your brain to get out of here—fast.

Before he gets round to telling you that he's married, or only in the market for a Friday night girl when he's in London. Or checks that you're on the Pill...

Suddenly she felt very cold. And scared. At the same time knowing for certain she didn't want to hear whatever he had to say.

Remembering too the dream that had so suddenly and providentially woken her.

Bella, she thought with horror. Oh, God, I was dreaming about Bella…

Carefully, she edged across the bed and put her feet to the floor. Heart drumming, she collected up her scattered clothing and tiptoed into the other room, dressing quickly and clumsily, alert to any danger sound from the bedroom.

She even remembered there was a trick to the lock and opened the door to the corridor smoothly and silently.

Halfway down, the lift stopped and, for one frozen moment, she thought Zandor might have found some way to recall it, but the doors opened to reveal two girls in neat green uniforms with cleaning trolleys. They immediately apologised and pressed the button for her to continue her descent, but Alanna saw the swift knowing look they'd exchanged and felt she'd just lost a layer of skin.

In the street outside it was overcast and chilly enough for Alanna to huddle into her jacket as she tried to get her bearings and work out where she'd find the nearest bus stop or Tube station.

But as she hesitated, a black cab cruised to a halt beside her. Its light was off, but the middle-aged driver leaned across, frowning, and spoke to her.

'Bit early to be on your own, young lady. What's the trouble? Had a row with the boyfriend?'

Alanna bit her lip. 'Something like that,' she returned defensively.

'I'm on my way home,' he said, 'but if the Wandsworth direction's any good to you, I can drop you off somewhere.'

'That would be brilliant,' she accepted unsteadily.

He was as good as his word, setting her down at the end of her road and flatly refusing to take any payment.

'Glad to help, love. I hope someone would do the same for my daughter if they found her wandering around at this time of day.' He smiled at her. 'And make that fellow grovel.'

As it was Saturday, the other tenants were in no hurry to rise, so Alanna didn't have the usual fight for the bathroom. She turned up the temperature of the shower until it was only just bearable and scrubbed herself rigorously from head to toe as if it was possible to scald away his touch.

She only wished the same tactics could clear her memory. Make her feel clean again mentally as well as physically. Except it was too late for that. She'd behaved like a fool, and worse than a fool, and now she had to live with the consequences, she told herself shuddering.

Whatever they might be.

Drying her hair in front of her room's solitary mirror, she found she was studying her reflection with a kind of odd detachment. Trying to work out what it was that had prompted first the loathsome

Jeffrey Winton and then Zandor to regard her as fair game.

I must be giving off signals, she thought, biting her lip. Indicating somehow that I'm 'gagging for it', in the revolting phrase I heard one of the guys in my year at uni once use.

But I never thought it could ever apply to me. More proof of my total stupidity.

Because it was one of the reasons I was determined not to sleep around but to wait until I was in a loving, committed relationship.

Another serious reason being Bella, she thought, swallowing past the tightness in her throat as the word 'loving' stung at her brain.

Or that's what I told myself. Perhaps, in reality, it was just that I'd never been seriously tempted before.

But, as a result, I made a conscious decision not to go on the Pill, relying instead on my own self-control to keep me safe.

Which has always worked perfectly—until last night.

She took a deep breath. She had planned to work on a script this weekend, but knew she couldn't promise to give it her best if she stayed here alone, brooding. Thinking the unthinkable.

So—she'd find herself some company, the best in the world.

She dressed quickly in jeans and a loose cotton

top, then got out her leather shoulder bag, filling it with a spare shirt, a change of underwear, her night things, and, finally, the script.

She swallowed a cup of black coffee and a slice of toast, then, after stuffing everything she'd worn the previous evening into a garbage sack and depositing it in an outside bin, she set off for the railway station.

An hour later, she was walking up the lane towards her parents' cottage, noticing as she reached the gate that there was a 'Sold' sign on the house opposite.

She also discovered that instinct hadn't played her false. Although it was still early, her mother, clad in loose cotton trousers and a floral blouse, mug of tea in hand, was patrolling the front garden, ready to deal death and destruction to any weed unwise enough to raise its head among her flowers.

Alanna leaned on the gate. 'Hi, Ma,' she called lightly. 'Stand by to repel boarders.'

Mrs Beckett started, then hurried down the path, wreathed in smiles. 'Darling, what a lovely surprise. Daddy will be absolutely thrilled. He said last night it was time you came down again. The thought must have reached you on the ether.'

I wish, Alanna thought with a pang as she unlatched the gate and was received into her mother's embrace.

'He's about to put together some bacon sandwiches,' sad Mrs Beckett happily. 'I'll tell him to do a couple of extra rashers.'

'I've already had breakfast,' Alanna protested.

'Indeed.' She was swept by a comprehensive maternal glance. 'Then you'll have to manage another. You've obviously lost weight, and you're looking a little frayed round the edges, my love. In need of some TLC, I'd say.'

Alanna smiled back at her. 'OK, Mother, dear, I know when I'm beaten.'

As they walked round to the kitchen door, she added, 'I see the Eastwoods are moving. Isn't that rather unexpected?'

'Unexpected but understandable.' Mrs Beckett gave her a sideways glance. 'Have you still not heard from Bella?'

'No, not a word since she dropped out of uni.' Alanna paused. 'But, oddly enough, I was thinking about her quite recently.'

'Picking up the vibes, perhaps,' her mother said grimly. 'She's pregnant.'

Alanna halted. 'Again?' The word escaped her before she could stop it. 'Oh, Lord, I didn't mean that as it sounded.'

'Well, you're not the first to say it. Bob and Hester are distraught. And this time she intends to keep the baby.'

'So she and the father are together?'

Mrs Beckett gave her an old-fashioned look. 'For

that she'd have to know his identity,' she returned drily. 'That's why her parents are moving—to support her.' She sighed. 'Apparently it was someone she met at a party. She'd been drinking as usual and they didn't swap phone numbers or even names. And now she's messed up her life a second time— all for a one-night stand with a total stranger. Can you imagine?'

She threw open the back door and addressed her husband, busy at the stove. 'Harry, look what the morning breeze has blown in.'

She turned to Alanna. 'Well, give him a hug, darling. Don't just stand there as if you'd been pole-axed.'

CHAPTER EIGHT

YET POLE-AXED WAS exactly how she'd felt, Alanna remembered wryly, standing there her mother's sun-filled kitchen, already weighed down with guilt, and now hardly able to believe her ears.

She and Bella had been at school together, in the same year and the same class, but never that close although their parents were friends.

By sheer chance they'd also ended up at the same university, but there their paths had divided with Alanna reading English, while Bella had opted for History.

Their social lives were very different too. Alanna, naturally shy, had concentrated on work, while Bella, with her stunning blonde looks, had soon moved into the fast lane.

There she'd met Charlie Mountney, elder son of a viscount, already in his third year, and they'd instantly become an item.

'Well, I hope she has fun,' said Alanna's roommate bluntly. 'Because that's all it ever is with Charlie. After his Finals he's off to manage the family estate in Staffordshire and duly marry the girl next door.' She paused. 'If Bella's a mate of yours, a word of warning might not come amiss.'

'Oh, I think it might,' Alanna had returned lightly. 'I'm sure Bella knows what she's doing.'

But she'd been wrong, because only a few months later, Bella had suddenly dropped out of her course and disappeared, allegedly suffering from glandular fever, while Charlie was soon seen around campus with a pretty redhead from the second year.

'By all accounts, Bella was getting too intense,' said the roommate. 'And with no engagement in sight, she played the "I'm pregnant" card and Charlie said "Deal with it" and walked.'

She shrugged. 'She'll be back one of these days, sadder and wiser.'

But that hadn't happened and when Alanna arrived home for the summer vacation, she learned that Bella had indeed undergone a termination and subsequently lapsed into an acute depression, screaming at her anguished parents that Charlie was the only man she would ever love. Begging them to contact him and tell him so, and, this time, to make him believe it.

'But how can we?' Hester Eastwood had sobbed to Alanna's mother. 'It's obviously all over. She has to accept that and get on with her life.'

Yet, as Alanna had later discovered, this was easier said than done.

But at the time, she thought bitterly, smug little prig that I was, I actually wondered how Bella could have been such a fool. Taken such a risk with her future.

In fact, heaven help me, I treated her as a kind of Awful Warning.

Well, on that morning a year ago, she'd found out. Had become desperately, agonisingly aware that she'd been equally foolish—equally reckless. Equally lacking in any justification for her behaviour.

Because, for all she knew, she also could be about to break her parents' hearts with the news that, having had unprotected sex, she too was expecting a child by a complete stranger, with hard choices to be made that would affect them all for ever.

As for Bella, discharged from the clinic, she'd moved to London, found a job with a publicity outfit, and re-started the high life. Relations with her parents had remained strained however, as she openly blamed them for failing to talk her out of the termination.

As if anyone had been able to talk Bella out of anything.

Poor things, she'd thought then, only to realise as she sat at the kitchen table, struggling to eat her bacon sandwich and talk brightly about how work was going, that people in the village might be saying that about her own parents before long.

She'd endured nearly ten days of silent misery until, by some miracle, her period had arrived absolutely on time.

And as she wept tears of shamed relief she made

a vow that if, as it seemed, she couldn't resist temptation—or that, *a propos* Jeffrey Winton, she was giving out the wrong kind of vibes—she would from that moment on put herself quietly and firmly out of temptation's way and try to emit no vibes at all.

But the entire experience had left her feeling vulnerable, which was why she'd snatched at the chance of moving in with Susie.

Yet now, just when she'd thought it was safe to venture back into the real world, all this had to happen. By some cruel twist of Fate, Zandor had reappeared in her life—or at least on its periphery—and that only on a strictly temporary basis, she reminded herself with steely determination.

And his unexpected departure tonight had to be a good sign—an indication that, having been proved wrong, he would be taking no further interest in the Harrington family's entanglements.

Anyway, that was what she would hope, at the same time firmly quelling the faint quiver of apprehension deep within her, suggesting it might not be that simple.

And, more disturbingly, why this could be so.

'Tasty,' said Susie approvingly. 'In fact, very tasty indeed. Well done that girl.' She paused. 'That is, of course, if you're in it for the long haul, because it strikes me that Mr Gerard Harrington will take some getting to know, and it will cost you time and effort to find his secret side.'

Alanna poured herself more coffee. It would, she decided ruefully, have made life easier if Susie had been off playing squash as she often did on Sunday mornings so that the flat would be empty when Gerard insisted on carrying her bag from the car, as she'd known he would.

It had been a muted departure from the abbey. Neither Gerard's grandmother nor his mother had appeared at the breakfast table, and Alanna had waited in the hall while he dashed upstairs to say his goodbyes, and accordingly was caught there by Joanne insisting they swap home and work addresses, telephone numbers and emails.

'You're part of the family now so we must keep in touch,' she'd declared ebulliently.

The mess deepens, Alanna thought dismally, as she complied. And Joanne's going to be so disappointed.

During the drive back to London, she'd reiterated her insistence that there should be no further announcements, public or personal, of the supposed engagement, and Gerard had reluctantly agreed, protesting that she should at least have an engagement ring.

'Perhaps,' Alanna conceded. 'For the time being. But only to be worn when we're with your family.'

Which, she hoped devoutly, would not be any

time soon. And what she really needed was to extricate herself from the entire situation before it became any worse.

The first potential complication, of course, had been Susie, at home and waiting to be introduced. But, to Alanna's relief, Gerard, while accepting coffee, had smilingly declined Susie's subsequent cheerful offer of pot-luck lunch and departed, no doubt to mull over the events of the weekend, and its aftermath. As she would have to do herself.

Now she said composedly, 'I doubt he has one.' Apart from this joint effort, she thought, before adding, 'Anyway the keeping of secrets is no big deal for the Harringtons as I found out after five minutes with his cousin Joanne. Lovely, but a self-appointed mine of information.'

'Everybody has something to hide,' said Susie darkly. 'And this particular Harrington is no exception, mark my words.'

'Duly marked.' Alanna hesitated. 'As for the long haul—that's still debatable.'

'The weekend something of a strain?'

'Something,' Alanna agreed.

'The grandmother more old witch than good fairy?'

'Along those lines.'

Not that it would have mattered too much if she'd been in love with Gerard, she reflected, because then she'd have been prepared to fight for him tooth and nail, whatever Niamh Harrington—or any other family member—threw at her.

So, her pride had been damaged. So what? Was that frozen look of Mrs Harrington's face sufficient justification for tangling herself in this web of deceit?

Zandor's abrupt departure was a totally different matter, an achievement which made any kind of inconvenience worthwhile. That was what she had to remember.

She drew a deep breath, then said more briskly, 'But, for the time being, I really need to concentrate on work, which has its own tricky side just now. For instance, tomorrow I have to turn down a good script by an unknown to make room for a lousy one from a Big Name. A prospect I don't relish, and a battle that I really needed to win.'

Susie grimaced. 'Sounds ominous.'

Alanna nodded. 'It feels it too. The fact is, I have to establish myself more firmly in the editorial team, in case the company is bought out. And I think Hetty would have fought a better fight for Gina Franklin than I did—and come out victorious at the end of it,' she added despondently.

'Don't run yourself down.' Susie gave her a light punch on the shoulder. 'Put the weekend and its negatives behind you, and decide that from now on everything's coming up roses.'

Dodgy things, roses, Alanna thought wryly, often

arriving with a full complement of greenfly, rust, black spot and the odd thorn. But she could only hope for the best.

Monday's interview over lunch with Gina Franklin went far better than she could have hoped. The girl was obviously deeply disappointed, but Alanna managed to convince her that the rejection was solely on economic grounds, and because she still believed the book would sell, recommended an up and coming literary agency, hungry for new talent.

However, when she got back to the office, she found a palpable feeling of tension in the air.

'Bookworld has just gone online saying TiMar International have bid for us, so watch this space,' Sadie from Non-Fiction informed her at the water cooler. She snorted. 'Nice if we'd heard it first.'

Alanna frowned. 'Who are they?'

'Big, still growing, and based in America,' said Sadie. 'Their main interests are in television and other media and their production companies have put out loads of successful series drama and documentaries, but they also have sidelines in the tourist industry and other stuff.

'Now, they're apparently looking to extend into book publishing, which may or may not be good news for us.' She sighed. 'I guess we'll just have to wait and see.'

'Yes,' Alanna said slowly. 'I suppose we will.'

But whatever happens, she told herself determinedly, as she returned to her desk, I intend to remain part of the team.

The rumour mill was in full flow during the week, but Alanna kept her head down and her mind strictly on the scripts in front of her, refusing to be distracted by speculation on the effects of the take-over, even when she was told that members of the TiMar board were arriving the following Monday for negotiations.

It's all in the lap of the gods, she told herself, and fussing about it will do no good at all, especially when I have more personal problems to consider.

As she'd left work the night before, she'd found Gerard waiting at reception.

'Hi. I was hoping we could have dinner together.'

'Not this evening.' She indicated the leather case hanging from her shoulder. 'I have some preliminary reads to do asap.'

'Then how about an equally preliminary drink.' He smiled at her then added quietly, 'We really need to talk.'

How quickly things could change, she thought without pleasure. A week ago, I'd probably have accepted like a shot.

She made herself smile back. 'Then a drink it is.'

When they were settled in a nearby wine bar, she sipped her spritzer and asked, 'What's so urgent?'

Gerard examined the colour of his own glass of

Cabernet Sauvignon, and frowned. 'My aunt Caroline. She's telephoned me twice and called in at the shop, wanting to know why our engagement has not yet featured in the broadsheets. Hoping it means we've come to our senses and rethought the whole thing.'

'I see.' Alanna paused. 'And what did you say?'

'That we needed to tell your parents first, but they were currently abroad.' He pulled a face. 'Another lie. I seem to have an aptitude for them.'

She bit her lip. 'Maybe it's time for the truth.'

'In which case we'll both look like idiots, and I'll be back at square one.' He shook his head. 'No, I think we should stick to our agreement, which, of course, means you having a word with your family. Are you seeing them any time soon?'

She hesitated. 'I'd planned to go down this weekend. That's why I'm trying to clear my decks.'

'That's a great idea,' he approved eagerly. 'Shall I come with you?'

'Good God, no.' She saw by his expression that she'd spoken too vehemently, and tried to temper her response. 'I'm sorry, but at the moment, they barely know you exist. Only that I've been seeing someone. I—I'd need to—to prepare the ground first.'

'Well, you know best.' He paused again. 'However, Aunt Caroline has also invited us to dinner next week. Friday or Saturday, she suggests. What do you think?'

That I'd rather dive head-first into a pond of piranhas...

Aloud, she said slowly, 'Well—that's very kind of her as well as rather unexpected. I can manage both evenings, so you decide.'

'Then let's make it Saturday. But we'll need to go shopping first.'

'I can do that. What would she prefer—flowers or chocolates?'

He shook his head. 'I meant shopping for a ring. She'll expect you to be wearing one.'

'I suppose so.' She thought for a moment, then nodded. 'And I will be. My grandmother left me her engagement ring, an opal and diamond cluster. It's in my bedroom at home, so I'll bring it back with me.'

'I'm quite prepared to buy you something suitable,' he began, but she stopped him.

'Not as things are,' she said firmly, and, as he hesitated, hoped with all her heart that he wouldn't reply, 'But they may change.'

But all he said was, 'Fine, we'll play it your way,' and left what she knew was 'For the time being,' hovering in the ether.

There was an editorial meeting on Friday afternoon which dragged on interminably, thanks to Louis who was clearly hell-bent on establishing himself as the future head of fiction under any new regime and turned even the most minor of decisions into a full debate.

So Alanna, fuming, was forced to change her plans and catch the Saturday morning train instead.

It was promising to be a beautiful weekend, warm and sunny with only the slightest of breezes, and as she walked up from the station, she felt the tensions of the past week gently slipping away.

As she walked up the path to the cottage, she became aware of voices in the back garden. It was no surprise to find visitors. Her mother and father, after all, joined fully in village life, so she made sure she was smiling dutifully as she rounded the house and saw them sitting with their guest at the table on the lawn, with coffee much in evidence.

Saw—and stopped dead, her shocked mind in freefall as she registered the identity of the newcomer, now rising politely to his feet, tall and lithe in faded jeans and a black polo shirt, his silver eyes glinting as they skimmed over her absorbing every detail of the sleeveless white blouse she'd teamed with a brief button-through skirt in dark green linen.

'Alanna, darling,' her mother greeted her buoyantly. 'Come and meet Mr Varga. He saw us in the front garden and stopped his car to ask for directions. We got talking—and here we are.'

Zandor said softly, 'But, amazingly, I believe that your daughter and I have already met—quite recently at a party, wasn't it? But perhaps you've forgotten.'

She managed to keep her voice steady. 'On the contrary, Mr Varga, I remember you perfectly well.'

She walked slowly forward. 'But what on earth are you doing in this locality?'

'House-hunting,' he said, and she felt her steps falter.

Before she could stop herself, she said hoarsely, 'You have to be joking.'

'Alanna.' Her father spoke reprovingly. 'Mr Varga is perfectly serious.'

She sank, flushing, onto the remaining chair, numbly accepting the coffee her mother had poured for her, praying at the same time that the cup would not rattle on its saucer and betray the fact that her hand was shaking.

She struggled to sound calm. 'I meant—why here, in deepest Sleepyville, of all unlikely places?'

Zandor shrugged, unruffled. 'Let's just say I'm tired of living out of a suitcase,' he said, his ironic glance reminding her that she'd seen the evidence of this for herself a year before.

She looked back at him defiantly. 'I'd have thought London would be your preferred habitat.'

'I'll have a place there too, but I plan to divide my time.' Zandor glanced round, drawing a deep, appreciative breath. 'Especially on weekends like this.'

'Mr Varga is on his way to view Leahaven Manor,' Mrs. Beckett put in. 'But he must have taken a wrong turning. It's easily done.'

I'll drink to that, Alanna thought grimly and swallowed a mouthful of coffee.

'But how strange that you and Alanna should already have encountered each other,' her father said cheerfully. 'And at a party, too, which is really good news.' He turned to his wife. 'For a while we were afraid she was turning into a total recluse, weren't we, darling?'

Just when I believed things couldn't get any worse, thought Alanna, smothering a groan.

She forced a smile. 'Dad, that's a total exaggeration, and you know it.'

'We know what we've seen with our own eyes, as well as what Susie told us,' Mr Beckett retorted robustly. 'That this past year, you've hardly bothered with a social life, never going out in the evenings and spending nearly every weekend down here.' He shook his head. 'So unlike yourself, sweetheart. Almost as if you were hiding.'

'It was just extra-busy at work,' she interrupted hastily, before he could offer any more damaging revelations. 'And with all this talk of a take-over, I felt I needed to demonstrate my commitment. Make sure I kept my job. You know that.'

'Ah, but you know what they say about all work and no play,' Zandor said softly. He smiled with great charm. 'Although no one could ever describe you as dull.'

Why was he doing this? she asked herself fiercely. And what in hell were my parents thinking of to allow a complete stranger into their home like this, whatever the pretext?

Oh, God, she thought, if they only knew how we really met. How I made a total fool of myself, behaving like a complete slut, and risking my entire future as well as their peace of mind into the bargain. It doesn't bear thinking about.

But he wouldn't be sitting here drinking coffee, that's for sure.

Her mother was speaking. 'I'm sure you'll like the manor, Mr Varga. Late Georgian and a little jewel.' She sighed. 'It's sad that Colonel Winslow decided to sell, but he was already a widower when poor Toby was killed in Iraq, and I suppose he felt he had nothing to stay for.'

'Of course,' Zandor said quietly. 'Has he moved locally?'

'No, to Australia. His daughter Clare is married to a sheep farmer in New South Wales and there are grandchildren now. They've been trying to persuade him to join them for ages.'

She paused. 'But you mustn't think it's an unhappy house, because I promise you it's not. It's full of good family memories.'

He smiled at her. 'You are quite a saleswoman, Mrs Beckett. Would you care to continue the good work and accompany me to the viewing? I'd value a female perspective.'

'I'd have loved to,' she said regretfully. 'But it's

the village art show this afternoon and Harry and I are going down to the hall presently to help set up.'

'And possibly prevent internecine warfare,' her husband added with a chuckle. He hesitated. 'But Alanna's not involved, so she could go with you—deliver the woman's angle. And we could meet up in The King's Arms later to hear the verdict over a ploughman's.'

'Naturally, I would be glad of her company.' Zandor turned to her. 'If, of course, she is willing.'

The words seemed to hover in the air...

Alanna said tautly, 'I'm sure you don't need outside help to make your decisions, Mr Varga.'

'Oh, please,' he said. 'When we met before, it was Zandor or even—Zan. Or have you forgotten?'

He allowed the silence to lengthen, then added, 'But this time I would welcome another opinion, besides ensuring that I don't get lost again.'

She was aware that her parents were watching her expectantly. Her mother, in particular, might indeed have had 'Eligible Bachelor' tattooed across her forehead, she decided bitterly, concealing a shudder.

Because I'm the one who seems to be lost, and there's nothing I can do about it.

From somewhere, she produced a smile. 'Well we can't risk that,' she said. *Or you might move in.* 'So, shall we go?'

And somehow walked with him out to where his car was waiting.

CHAPTER NINE

As HE STARTED the car, she said icily, 'Do you really have as much as a passing interest in Leahaven Manor, or are you just stalking me?'

'The agents' details are in the glove compartment,' he returned as they drove off.

'That isn't what I asked.'

'Then, yes, I do have an interest,' he said. 'Quite a strong one. Although I can see you object to the idea of having me as a neighbour.'

'I can manage to maintain an adequate distance,' she said. 'Even if you have managed to charm my mother and father.'

'And even though we're going to be related by marriage? Something your parents appear unaware of,' he went on musingly. 'I dropped Gerard's name casually into the conversation and got no reaction whatsoever. I found that strange. I also note you're not wearing a ring.'

'Well, please don't concern yourself,' she returned curtly. 'All that is due to change very soon. We're simply waiting for the right moment.'

'Of course,' Zandor said cordially. 'Just as you did last weekend. Now, why didn't I think of that?'

She didn't venture a response, just sat staring bleakly at the passing countryside.

In spite of herself, she was impressed by the power of the Lamborghini and, more annoyingly, by his effortless ability to handle it through the narrow lanes. Not to mention his newly acquired gift of finding his way without hesitation, she thought bitterly.

Eventually, she broke the silence. 'How did you find out where my family live? From Gerard, I suppose, or Joanne,' she added bitterly, although she couldn't remember mentioning the village by name to either of them.

He shrugged a shoulder. 'It wasn't too difficult,' he returned.

Which left her none the wiser but made her wonder whether it was his wish to see the manor which had prompted him to seek her out, or the other way round.

Whatever, she could not allow it to matter, she told herself with determination. Because he would eventually get tired of this cat and mouse game he was playing. She had to believe that.

Just as she had to assure herself that her mock-engagement would soon be over, leaving her free of all the Harrington clan—a moment that couldn't arrive too quickly to suit her.

Free also to meet someone and develop a relationship which might ripen into real love. A man, with whom there'd be no shameful back history to regret, and whom she'd want to introduce to her parents.

And who would not bear the remotest resemblance to the man seated beside her, in apparent control of the situation as well as the car.

As for now, when her mother began to ask the inevitable gentle questions, she would simply laugh and say that Zandor Varga was definitely not her type, besides having love interests on most of the continents of the known world. Currently someone called Lili…

Which was no more than the truth, she added defensively. And the truth would set her free. Somehow.

To add to her troubles, the estate agent waiting on the gravel sweep in front of the house was Jerry Morris, now a partner in his father's firm, but whose relentless pursuit of her during one summer vacation she'd finally ended with a hard kick on his shins.

His eyes now narrowed speculatively and without warmth when he saw her, suggesting this would be a juicy item to share with the lounge bar mob in the King's Head tonight.

But he was brisk and businesslike as he led the way to the front door with its pillared portico.

Alanna hung back a little, admiring the warmth of the manor's red brick and its clean classic lines, so like the pictures of the ideal house she'd drawn as a child, apart, of course, from the third storey attics which had housed the servants.

My dreams, she thought wryly, were never that grand.

And still aren't, she added, her lips tightening as she followed the two men into a well-proportioned hall with a black and white tiled floor and an elegant staircase curving gently upwards to the left.

All the furniture had been removed and there was already the faint mustiness of disuse in the empty rooms, but no discernible tang of damp.

Zandor said little as they explored the ground floor, but took his time, the silver eyes sombre as they observed the discoloured rectangles on the walls where pictures including family portraits must have once hung, the views from the tall uncurtained windows, and the vacant expanse of oak shelves in the Colonel's former library at the back of the house.

A green baize door led to the large old-fashioned kitchen with its adjacent scullery and pantries, as well as a boot room and what had been used as the gun room.

'All this will need updating, of course, but we feel this is reflected in the price,' Jerry Morris said brightly. 'The door ahead of you opens straight into the stable yard and fuel stores, and there's an archway which leads to the kitchen garden and a small orchard.'

He paused. 'Do you have horses, Mr Varga?'

'One, but I plan to have more.'

'Excellent,' was the hearty reply. 'Now for the

bedrooms, six in all on the first floor, one en suite, and another used in the past as a nursery.' His gaze flickered towards Alanna. 'Shall we pop up and have a look?'

I am popping nowhere, thought Alanna. She said coolly, 'I think I'd rather have a stroll outside,' and waited while Jerry made a business of unlocking the rear door.

Outside, she paused for a moment, steadying the odd flurry of her breathing, as she stared across at the empty loose boxes, visualising them occupied, with inquisitive, hopeful heads observing her approach with a handful of apple or carrot.

Altogether too much imagination, that's your problem, she told herself as she turned away. That's why you were mentally redecorating those rooms in clear pastels, and choosing retro cabinets and a massive central table for the kitchen, refashioning it into the heart of the house, when, in reality, the transformation was not hers to make.

She found the kitchen garden sadly neglected and overgrown as she wandered down its central path. Dad would have a wonderful time conducting a salvage operation, she thought, pausing to pick a sprig of mint and roll it between her fingers, inhaling its fragrance. Pity he won't get the chance.

She paused for a moment, looking back and sighing faintly. Because it was indeed a lovely house, spacious but not overwhelming, needing only some tender loving care to make it spectacular again.

But Zandor was a man living his life on a here today, gone tomorrow basis, and would have neither the time nor the patience to restore the manor to its former glory.

He'd want instant results—somewhere totally ready for occupation, and with more show than substance, she decided as she opened the wrought iron gate into the orchard.

This at least was surviving well, promising a good crop of apples in a couple of months' time. But who would be here to pick them?

The grass felt dry and springy under her feet as she walked slowly, lifting her face to the sun dappling through the clustering leaves. Some of the trees bore faint labels—Cox, Worcester and Bramley—while, at the far end, the largest tree, old now and bare of fruit, had a wooden swing attached by chains to one of its thick gnarled branches.

Toby and Clare would have played here, she thought sadly, and the swing had been left waiting for Toby's children in their turn—except an ambush in a dusty desert town had destroyed that possibility, turning a family home into an empty shell.

But it wouldn't stay like that. It couldn't. In time, another generation of children would come flying down the orchard, bickering over who would have the first turn.

She could almost see them—call out to them—except for the sudden inexplicable tightness in her throat and the unwanted sting of tears in her eyes.

You fool, she thought fiercely. You stupid, pathetic *idiot*...

As if she'd spoken aloud, a blackbird rocketed up from the sheltering grass with a startled flap of wings and took refuge in a neighbouring tree.

And, in the next instant, she heard the quiet sound of her name.

She turned, defensive and resentful, to find Zandor only a few feet away. Realising that, unlike the blackbird, she'd been too lost in ridiculous dreaming to be aware of his approach.

She said curtly, 'You didn't spend much time on the bedrooms.'

'I saw what I needed to see.'

Just as he was seeing her now—his gaze uncomfortably searching. He took a step nearer and altogether too close for comfort, she thought, damning that betraying sparkle of tears.

'What's the matter.'

'Nothing.' She lifted her chin. 'If we're done here, perhaps we could leave.'

'Why the hurry?'

'For one thing Jerry—Mr Morris—may have other genuine clients waiting to look round.'

'Ah,' he said softly. 'Then you have decided the manor is not for me.'

'I think we both know that.' She hesitated. 'This is a family house, a place to put down roots, and you're very much a bird of passage.'

'Didn't you hear me say I was tired of my suitcase?'

Alanna shrugged. 'I've also heard it said that leopards don't change their spots. So, how long before you start packing again?'

His eyes narrowed. 'Is this why you're angry with me? Because you believe that after our night together, I simply walked away? Moved on?'

'I,' she said, 'was the one who left.'

'And you think I accepted that?' He shook his head. 'You're so wrong, Alanna. I went to find you as soon as I got back from the States. I traced the bookshop, but it had changed hands and the new manager knew nothing about a girl assistant at a book signing.'

He paused. 'As I had no other information, I didn't know where else to start looking.'

She made herself ignore the strange lurch of sensation deep inside her.

She thought—*He came looking for me...*

She steeled herself. 'Clearly you take rejection badly.'

'We had unprotected sex,' he said, too softly. 'I did not relish being left in ignorance of any possible consequences.'

'Luckily, there weren't any,' she threw back at

him, closing her mind to those terrible ten days of uncertainty. 'But if there'd been a problem, I'd have dealt with it. Nor would I have *relished* any attempt at intervention.'

She knew at once that she'd made a mistake, even before she saw the icy glitter in his eyes and the dark flush staining his cheekbones.

And before his hands grasped her shoulders, pulling her to him without gentleness or finesse, or as his mouth descended on hers, parting her lips in a merciless demand that send her body and senses reeling.

The same instinct told her not to make him angrier by struggling, but to stand and endure, hands helpless at her sides, her body trapped between his and the rough bark of the tree behind her. To wait until the storm passed and reason returned to the spinning world.

Which was not soon.

Because, in spite of herself, she found the pressure of his mouth and the invasion of his tongue, however ruthless, was igniting a spark of response as unexpected as it was unwelcome.

And that this same spark was suddenly, dangerously flaring into urgency as the heat of his skin penetrated the layers of clothing between them, from her breasts to her belly and thighs, giving the disturbing illusion that they were both naked.

As they had been that other unforgotten and unforgettable time...

A tiny moan escaped her, half protest, half need, to be lost in the deepening of his kiss as it changed from anger to the raw insistence of passion.

Almost of their own volition, her arms were sliding round his waist, her fingers splaying across his back to hold him close, then closer still as if she was seeking to be joined to him. Once again absorbed and made part of him.

Which could not—must not happen.

She knew that as clearly as she needed air to breathe. Knew that disaster beckoned while she stayed in his arms. If she stayed there...

If she allowed his fingers to slip from her shoulders, as they were doing now, and unfasten the buttons on her blouse, releasing the rounded softness of her breasts from the lace confines of her bra.

If she let him cup them in his hands, while his thumbs gently stroked her rosy nipples to aching, irresistible arousal.

Wrong—all so wrong...

The words seemed to sigh in her brain as if logic and reason still retained any power over her responses.

Zandor bent his head, taking each swollen peak in turn into his mouth, laving them softly—devastatingly with his tongue, while his hand slid down to her waist to begin, slowly and deliberately, to free the buttons on her skirt.

She seemed to be enclosed with him in a cocoon of golden stillness, its quietude disturbed only by the rustle of the leaves above their heads, the far-off cooing of a wood pigeon and the sudden husky whisper of their quickening breathing.

And then, like a swift blow across the senses, came the distant voice of Jerry Morris, calling from the gateway. 'Mr Varga? Are you there? Because I'd like to lock up now, unless, of course, you want to go round the house again. Mr Varga?'

Alanna felt Zandor's hands fall away from her. Was aware of him turning sharply to stand in front of her, shielding her half-clothed body with his own as he called back, his voice faintly unsteady, 'No, that's fine. I'll be right with you.'

Heard him draw a deep harsh breath, then watched him walk away unhurriedly through the clustering trees, leaving her to deal, hands shaking, with her disordered clothing.

And to tell herself that the interruption had mercifully saved her from yet another potential disaster.

The worst of it being that in just a few brief moments, he'd transformed her from hostility to being ready and so much more than willing, and that he'd known it.

His for the taking, she thought, swallowing past the tightness in her throat, and he could have stripped her and indeed taken her right there on the soft grass without her making the least effort to prevent him.

Which made her—what? she wondered, bitterly conscious that her ungiven, unfulfilled body was now one desperate scream of frustration. Some kind of female sex toy, totally controlled by her hormones and devoid of self-respect, for him to use and discard as the mood took him?

Or was her behaviour just a temporary aberration, nothing more? Which was what she'd fought to believe throughout those endless months. Finally telling herself that she'd succeeded.

Well now she knew differently. Knew that Zandor was somehow *there*—in her skin, her bones, her blood. An incredible—terrifying—part of herself that she would need emotional surgery to remove before she could get on with the rest of her life.

Beginning now. At the moment when she would have to face him again.

Her clothing restored to decency, she walked back to the stable yard and found a gravelled path leading round the side of the house to the parking area.

Jerry Morris's car had gone and only Zandor was waiting, a solitary figure behind the wheel of the Lamborghini, staring into space, his dark face remote.

Hands balled into defensive fists at her sides, she walked slowly towards the car, watching him lean across and open the passenger door for her. Knowing that, without her phone or wallet, both in the bag she'd left at the cottage, she had no choice other than to join him.

At the same time trying to quell, or at least conceal, the tremors of uncertainty quivering inside her. Recognising and despising her own weakness.

He sat beside her, unmoving, his face bleak, his body taut. When he spoke, his voice was husky.

'Please believe—I—did not intend this.'

'What in particular?' She was fumbling with the seat belt. 'Deceiving my parents, forcing me to accompany you here, or letting Jerry Morris, the biggest scandalmonger in a hundred miles, catch you stripping me?'

She hardly recognised the ugliness in her voice. The ugliness in the actual words. But told herself it was the only possible response.

'He saw nothing,' he said quietly. 'And if I've deceived your parents, I am not the only one.'

He paused. 'But we still need to talk, Alanna, and it seemed to me that this could be the right place. Neutral territory.'

'There is no right place,' she said thickly. 'And this conversation you're still trying to foist on me is never going to happen. Because I don't want to hear it, or anything else you may have to say.'

'Perhaps it's your own words I wish to discuss. Or have you forgotten them? Shall I remind you?'

'*No.*' The word was almost violent, her throat closing in panic. 'That's all past and gone.' She took a breath, steadied her voice. 'How many times must I tell you? So believe it now. And finally accept that I never want to set eyes on you again. Ever.'

'That,' he said almost musingly, 'may cause problems, and in the near future too.'

She hunched a shoulder, staring ahead of her. Refusing to turn her head. To look at him...

'At family gatherings?' She injected a note of contempt into her tone. 'I wouldn't say you were the prize guest with any of your relatives. Especially if I tell Gerard what you tried today.'

He said harshly, 'And what do you imagine he would say—or do?'

'Because you're the big boss and you might fire him?' She hunched a shoulder. 'He can always get another job.'

'Of course,' he said. 'As he and I both know. But he's always preferred the easy option. And you're not the one to change his mind, believe me.'

'I wouldn't believe it if you told me today was Saturday.' She swallowed past the tightness in her throat. 'The biggest mistake of my life so far was to accept your help that night at the bookshop.

'But it will never happen again. And I only wish I could somehow erase my existing notch on your bedpost, but I certainly won't be adding another to it, not even if you were to—to save me from drowning.'

Her voice came to a shaking halt and was followed by a silence somehow louder than any words could ever have been.

When he eventually spoke: 'Quite a speech,' he observed softly. 'And now I'll drive you back to the safety of your village—unless you wish your embargo on my services to begin at once. No?' The smile he sent her was like a knife blade held to her skin. 'How very wise. But understand one thing—that this is not the end.'

And he started the car.

The King's Head was crowded as it usually was at weekends, but her parents, together with some other Art Show devotees, had bagged a large table by the window.

'We haven't ordered the food yet, but we've started a tab at the bar, so get yourself a drink,' her mother said, smiling. She looked round. 'Where's Mr Varga—Zandor?'

Alanna managed to keep her voice casual. 'Oh, he was clearly in a hurry to get back to London.'

'But what did he think of the house?' her father asked.

She shrugged. 'Probably that it needs work.'

She glanced round the table. 'Any more drinks for anyone?'

There were no takers, so she threaded her way between the tables to the only empty space at the busy bar, and leaned there against the polished wood, staring with unseeing eyes at the row of optics in front of her. Rather as she'd sat silent and motionless, thankfully concealing the fact that she was shaking inside, for the duration of that seemingly endless return journey.

Or that it would take very little for her to burst into tears.

She'd been sorely tempted when they reached the pub to wait until Zandor had driven off and then disappear back to the cottage, where she could fall apart in peace and privacy, but she knew her absence would only lead to far trickier questions, and it would be best to deal with her parents' enquiries by providing answers that were simple, direct and immediate.

Also, she thought, it was often easier to lose oneself in a crowd, and pinned on another smile as she ordered a ginger beer shandy.

As she turned, glass in hand, she almost bumped into Jerry Morris, his face flushed and angry. A problem she had not foreseen, she realised, her heart sinking.

'What the hell did you say to him?' he demanded thickly. 'Are you trying to drive me out of business?'

'I don't know what you're talking about.' She tried to pass but he put a hand on her arm.

'Your billionaire boyfriend—that's what. I had

it nailed. It was a done deal, for God's sake, and now he's called to say he won't be making an offer after all.'

'Then perhaps you're not quite the super salesman you think.' Alanna wrenched herself free, glaring back at him.

'In the same way that he's not my boyfriend—or a billionaire.'

'You think we didn't check him out?' He gave a contemptuous snort. 'Do me a favour. So, the last thing I expected was a time-waster. And if you're not involved, why were you hiding away with him at the bottom of the orchard?'

His mouth straightened into a sneer. 'Unless, of course, you were the real time-waster—leading him on, then coming over all Little Miss Touch-Me-Not at the last minute. After all, he wouldn't be the first guy you've fooled like that,' he added with heavy meaning.

'Dear me.' She lifted her chin, anger adding a dangerous spark to the other emotions churning inside her. 'Perhaps I should be issued with a government health warning. But fortunately my fiancé doesn't seem to share your views.'

'Fiancé?' His eyes shifted suspiciously to her bare left hand. 'You said the Varga guy wasn't your boyfriend.'

'Nor is he.' Too late to draw back now, she thought. All her good intentions blown to smithereens. So—in for a penny, in for a pound, and Gerard at least would be pleased. Wouldn't he?

She took a deep breath. 'I'm actually engaged to his cousin, who already has a house, older and larger than the manor—in case you had other hopes.'

And, like the manor, one of the last places on earth I'd ever want to inhabit, she added silently, resolutely consigning the fantasies of an hour ago to some mental waste bin.

Because breaking the news to her parents and Susie, and to colleagues at work, would bring quite enough problems.

But she needed to prove to Zandor, once and for all, that he was completely wrong.

And that this was, indeed, the end of something that should never—ever—have begun.

CHAPTER TEN

As Alanna got ready for bed that night, it occurred to her that, for the first time, it would be a relief to get the train back to London the following evening.

Not unexpectedly, her parents were stunned, and not in a good way, to learn she was apparently committed to a man they'd never met or even heard of, and clearly dissatisfied by her admittedly lame explanations.

But, if they had to know, it was surely better coming from her than via Jerry the human Tweet, she decided grimly. And at least he'd been deterred from spreading any juicy stories about her presence at the manor, or being found 'hiding away' with Zandor in the orchard.

That however was small consolation for having the minutiae of where she and Gerard had met, and how and particularly when, gone over in agonising detail.

'So this Gerard Harrington is actually Mr Varga's cousin?' her mother repeated incredulously. 'What on earth must he have thought when we never mentioned him?'

Alanna bit her lip. 'That it had all happened rather quickly, and I was simply waiting for the right moment to tell you.' Which was as near the truth as she was prepared to go.

'I'd hardly describe any part of this situation as simple,' Mr Beckett said drily. 'Are you quite sure you know what you're doing?'

'You've always said that as soon as you saw Mummy, you knew,' Alanna said defensively. 'Why shouldn't it happen to me too?'

'Because your mother took rather longer to persuade,' he retorted drily. 'That's how it usually goes.'

'Well, not this time.' She tried to smile. 'I hoped you'd be pleased.'

'When you can't show us a photograph—even one of those selfie things on your phone?' Her mother sighed. 'It all seems—so odd. Especially when I thought…' She broke off, flushing a little, then her gentle mouth tightened. 'Of course, you know what people will say.'

'Then they couldn't be more wrong,' Alanna assured her quickly. 'And we certainly won't be getting married any time soon.' *Or ever…*

'His parents? You've met them, I presume?'

Next big snag, thought Alanna, groaning silently.

Aloud, she attempted brightness. 'Well, yes. His mother's a widow who lives in Suffolk.'

'And what does she think about this sudden decision?'

Alanna shrugged, wondering who could possibly know Meg Harrington's opinion on anything.

'That we're adults who can make up our own minds,' she returned. 'Darlings, it will all work out. I promise you.'

'Well, we can only hope so.' Her mother paused. 'Mr Varga and your Gerard, I suppose, being cousins, they're quite alike.'

'Not in the slightest. Absolute chalk and cheese,' Alanna denied with rather more force than she'd intended.

'I see,' said Mrs Beckett thoughtfully.

And there, on the surface anyway, it was left.

But if Alanna hoped bedtime would give her the opportunity to relax, she soon found she was wrong.

Instead, she spent a wretched night, tossing and turning, her body's turmoil reflecting the chaos of her emotions.

They said confession was good for the soul, she thought miserably, but that must only be when you could tell the truth, the whole truth and nothing but the truth.

Yet, in her case, that was still impossible.

And it was all her own fault.

Because, that night in London, she could have called the lift and gone down to the waiting cab, to resume her normal existence.

Because, at the abbey she could have told Gerard to sort out his own marital problems, and walked away.

Because, she could also have found some excuse—a headache, plans of her own, or urgent scripts to be read—in fact *anything*, for God's sake, to avoid accompanying Zandor to the manor, or anywhere else for that matter.

And, once there, why hadn't she waited staidly downstairs in the hall while he completed his inspection of the bedrooms, like any sane person would have done, instead of drifting into the garden and allowing herself to be found indulging inexplicable fantasies in a disturbingly secluded spot?

But once found, why hadn't she dodged any potentially disastrous confrontation by looking at her watch, expressing concern about the time then leading the way briskly back to the car.

In fact, she groaned inwardly, why hadn't she followed any of those eminently sensible courses of conduct, thereby avoiding a load of grief?

That was what she couldn't understand or explain, least of all why she'd said what she did about a possible pregnancy, as if she was deliberately trying to provoke him.

Which was dangerous nonsense, especially in view of what had followed...

She turned over yet again, aware that her breathing had quickened, then sat up abruptly, pushing away the covers, before stripping the nightgown from her overheated body and tossing it to the floor.

Even so, just the Egyptian cotton sheet still seemed to be causing too much friction against her starkly sensitised flesh, her nipples erect and swollen, her thighs and belly taut with a tension as unfamiliar as it was unwelcome.

Because, for a shocked moment, she was back in the orchard, Zandor's mouth taking hers in passionate demand, his body harshly aroused against hers as his hands caressed her naked breasts, and then, as the night seemed to stand breathlessly, eternally still, she heard herself sigh, softly, achingly, as if, again, she was waiting for his possession.

Once more experiencing the glorious reality of his body sheathed in hers, every long rhythmic movement forcing her ever closer to the exquisite agony of culmination, then at last carrying her exultantly over the brink...

Gasping, she managed to break the spell, pressing horrified hands to her burning face, whispering that this was sheer delusion, a few shameful seconds of madness which she could not—would not allow to continue, and with implications she refused even to consider.

'I have to stop beating myself up about this,' she whispered. 'I've made it clear I want him out of my life and he's apparently accepted that. So what I need now is to erase him from my...'

She faltered suddenly aware that she'd been about to say *heart and mind*. But Zandor Varga had no place in her heart and never would have, so she swiftly substituted *memory* as a much safer option.

But tonight selective amnesia clearly needed some assistance. She slid out of bed and grabbed her elderly bathrobe from the back of the door before slipping quickly and quietly down the passage to the bathroom, and the cabinet where her mother kept a bottle of non-prescription sleeping pills for occasional use.

She hadn't much faith in their efficiency, but perhaps the mere act of swallowing the recommended dose was enough to slow down the mental treadmill which had her trapped, and eventually release her from it into a deep and thankfully dreamless sleep.

On the train, she called Gerard and outlined the new development, omitting any mention of Zandor's part in it, and telling him he could announce the engagement publicly, if he wished.

'Of course I do.' He sounded actually buoyant. 'Darling, you won't regret this, I promise.'

Oh, God, she thought wearily, as she rang off. That is so not true.

And now, of course, she had to face Susie.

Whose first response when she'd finished her halting explanation was, 'Wow.'

'And to think it seems like only a short time ago you were swearing blind that there was no engagement in sight,' she continued affably.

Alanna shifted uncomfortably. 'Well, things change.'

'Clearly.' Susie gave her an ironic look. 'But not usually so quickly. Don't forget what they say about repenting at leisure.'

'That,' said Alanna, feeling she was already drowning in repentance, 'refers to marriage, which quite definitely is not on the cards.'

'Depends who's dealing,' said Susie.

'Anyway,' Alanna went on, determinedly disregarding the last remark. 'That secret you said he was hiding. At least you know what it was now.'

Susie considered. 'No,' she said slowly. 'I don't think I do. Or you either. Not yet.'

And as the kitchen timer pinged, with Alanna staring after her, she went to fetch the bacon and egg flan she'd made for supper from the oven.

The office was already buzzing when Alanna arrived on Monday, and by the time she'd poured herself some fresh coffee from the dazzling machine in the kitchenette, she'd learned that meetings had been held all day Sunday, and since seven that morning, and that the deal was finally done.

Hawkseye Publishing was now officially part of the TiMar empire.

'And apparently it's business as usual and no redundancies, thank heavens,' said Jeanne, from the art department. 'Steve and I have just taken out the most horrendous mortgage on a new flat,' she added, shuddering. 'I don't know what we'd have done.'

She gave Alanna a friendly nudge. 'But you never had to worry. After all, you're Hetty's blue-eyed girl.'

Except, thought Alanna, that Hetty isn't here...

The official announcement was to be made in the boardroom at eleven, and everyone, according to Louis, wearing an air of smugness that was almost tangible, was expected to attend.

Business as usual, Alanna wondered wryly, as she joined the throng, or, for him, something rather better? Time would show.

It was standing room only, so she tucked herself into a corner.

'They say the big boss himself, the actual head of TiMar, is going to be here, hence the three-line whip,' the girl next to her confided in an excited whisper.

That explained all the last-minute repairs with mascara and lip pencil, plus the wafts of freshly applied scent reaching her from all sides, Alanna decided with faint amusement.

She was her usual muted self, in tailored black pants and a pale green shirt, her hair drawn back from her face and severely confined at the nape of her neck.

And then the door at the far end opened, and silence fell as a group of men entered, one of them slightly ahead of the rest, immaculately clad again in charcoal grey, his silk tie impeccably knotted, his dark hair tamed, and moving as if he owned the place—which of course he now did.

Alanna's lips parted in a soundless gasp, as she shrank further into her corner. For a moment, she thought she must be going crazy. That because Zandor had once more forced himself on her attention that weekend, she was somehow imposing his image on a complete stranger.

Except this was no stranger...

Trembling, she felt time slip backwards to that evening in SolBooks when he'd first walked in and smiled at her, as she hurried down the shop towards him. Reminding her how her entire body seemed to warm under his gaze, as if this had been an intensely intimate reunion rather than a first meeting.

And that, for one heart-stopping moment, they were the only two people in the universe.

A sweet madness that had turned her voice to a husk as they'd spoken together, exchanging conventionalities.

And which, above all else, had forced her to the incredible certainty that whispered—*So here he is—at last...*

Something she'd tried to banish from her mind ever since, like so much else about that encounter, yet now found herself recalling in every vivid, disturbing detail.

Which told her too, with fierce, churning excitement that, no matter how hard she'd tried, nothing had changed. The urgency that had taken her back into his arms that night at the hotel was as potent—as dangerous as ever. Its implications as far-reaching and life-transforming.

Finally acknowledging that all the denials—all the harsh words that she had used to protect herself were irrelevant.

Admitting at last what she'd always known. That on that evening—that night all those months ago—she had fallen deeply and hopelessly in love with him, the stranger called Zandor who'd admitted he would be gone in the morning, and for whom, she told herself, she'd been no more than just another girl in another bed.

Someone she'd never see again, and for whom she'd committed the ultimate act of self-betrayal...

A humiliation she could not bear to remember and had tried so hard to forget. But all in vain.

Because he hadn't simply shrugged and gone on his way, after all. He'd tried to find her. And but for Clive Solomon's retirement, he would probably have succeeded. And then—what?

She had no answer to that.

As it was, she'd constructed her own ugly version of events, cementing it with heartache and bitterness. Convincing herself she'd behaved with a reckless, unforgivable stupidity, which must never be allowed to occur again.

That she must at all costs keep him at bay.

And less than forty-eight hours ago, she believed her campaign had succeeded at last.

Only to discover now that she'd been fooling herself.

Realising that if he looked at her and smiled, she would surrender to the soul-shaking need inside her and run the length of this room to throw herself once more into his arms.

Zandor paused at the top of the long table, his eyes sweeping the hierarchy waiting on either side, before briefly scanning the lesser mortals crammed together at the far end.

Skimming her briefly with a glance like ice turned silver by a winter moon before moving on with silent indifference. Total finality.

At all costs? she thought, her nails digging into the palms of her hands as her throat tightened, painfully, uncontrollably. Had she ever, until this moment, reckoned up the price she might have to pay?

Or examined her feelings about him with any kind of honesty?

Not until now, was the bleak answer, when it was

far too late. And that was something she'd have to live with for the rest of her life.

Then, as the silence in the room seemed to stretch to screaming point: 'Good morning, ladies and gentlemen,' said Zandor Varga.

Her office had always been more of a cubbyhole than a sanctuary, but Alanna dived into it, and fell, shaking, into the chair behind her desk.

There'd been no escape, of course. She'd had to stand there, sheer willpower holding her upright, for the duration of his short speech, outlining his reasons for choosing Hawkseye Publishing, commending their successes but also making it clear there was room for improvement.

So business as usual was by no means a certainty, she thought, remembering the uneasy looks being exchanged by his audience.

But she knew only too well whose head would be the first to roll.

The only question was would he wield the axe himself, or get one of the suits who'd followed him into the boardroom to do it?

TiMar, she thought. Of course—Timon and Marianne, the amalgamation of his parents' names, which Joanne had confided to her. How could she not have seen it—not have guessed?

And Jerry Morris had been right. Zan was indeed a billionaire, probably several times over.

Zandor had said she might have problems airbrushing him out of her life, but how could she have guessed how all-encompassing they might be? Especially with a man she'd once accused of not taking rejection well?

At least I got that right, she thought, pain twisting inside her.

But, however flimsy the reason for her coming dismissal, there was no way she would seek reparation from a tribunal, even if such action was justified, because who knew what skeletons might come tumbling from the cupboard?

She might even find herself portrayed as Zandor's vengeful discarded mistress, she realised, dry-mouthed.

She glanced at the contents of her in-tray, then reached with an unsteady hand for the script she'd been working on. At least she could clear her desk before the inevitable happened. Behave correctly and with dignity, although heaven only knew what kind of a reference she could expect.

But she would deal with that when she had to.

She ate her lunchtime sandwich in seclusion, bitterly aware that acquiring a boss who was not only mega-wealthy, single and sex on legs would be the sole topic of conversation among her female colleagues.

By this time they probably knew his collar size, she thought, for a brief instant allowing herself to imagine the reaction if she tossed, *I've seen him naked* into the conversation.

It was the only marginally bright moment in an increasingly bleak afternoon, crowned by a summons from Louis just as she was about to leave.

So he was the executioner of choice, she thought, resisting an impulse to lie down and drum her heels, screaming.

But to her astonishment, he greeted her pleasantly and invited her to sit down.

'I think it's clear to us all that the new regime is going to be pretty tough,' he opined importantly, leaning back in his chair. 'And while we're obviously looking to expand our fiction range, we also need to build on our current successes.

'Which brings me to you. While I have not always agreed with your judgement, I cannot deny your editing skills and ability to get the best from the authors on your list.'

He paused. 'In view of that, I've decided to give you a very special assignment. As you know, Jeffrey Winton has decided on a change of direction in order to attract a younger readership. Naturally, he feels he'll need help in making such a complete switch, so, from now on, and at his own request, you'll be working exclusively with him.'

He nodded graciously. 'This is an exciting career move for you, Alanna, and will naturally warrant a slight increase in salary, which may improve once the partnership has been successfully established.'

He eyed her. 'So, what do you say?'

Alanna drew a breath. 'Just this.' She couldn't believe how calm she sounded. 'That there isn't enough money in the world to persuade me to having anything to do with that squalid little lech, let alone work with him.

'And don't tell me he hasn't tried it on with other girls,' she added contemptuously. 'Because I won't believe it. So, briefly, and for the record, the answer is no because I'm quite happy working as I am.'

His eyes narrowed. 'I'm afraid it isn't as simple as that. I will overlook, for the moment, the slur on a bestselling author's reputation. In return you must understand that the decision has come from the top.'

He nodded at her faint gasp. 'Your current authors have been reassigned to other editors, leaving you free to concentrate your efforts on Jeffrey's behalf.' He smiled. 'He tells me he is very much looking forward to your input.'

So this is how it's going to be done, Alanna thought, feeling sick. What's known as virtual dismissal, because Zandor of all people knew exactly what her response would be to this new scheme.

The cruelty of it took her breath away.

How could he? she asked herself desolately. Why

didn't he simply include me in the first staff cull? Because there's bound to be one.

'Then Mr Winton is going to be disappointed.' She rose. 'Because I refuse to be connected with this project in any way. And don't worry. My resignation will be on your desk before I leave tonight.'

'Aren't you being rather foolish?' Louis tried to sound concerned but his eyes were glinting. 'Publishing jobs are hard to come by, and you're turning down a promotion.' He tutted. 'That won't look well on your CV.'

Alanna shrugged. 'I'll take my chances.'

At the door, she paused. 'Oh, and, still on the record, Jeffrey Winton is not only vastly untalented, but a sleazy little slimeball and you're welcome to tell him so from me.'

'Unlikely,' he said. 'And I strongly advise you not to repeat such comments, unless you want to find yourself in court. On the whole, I'd say you had enough problems already—wouldn't you?' He paused. 'More immediately, after you've written your resignation, I suggest you clear your desk. You're a loose cannon, Alanna, as I always suspected, so why delay the inevitable?'

Somehow she managed to keep her tone light. 'Why indeed?' she agreed, and left him.

CHAPTER ELEVEN

'WHAT AM I going to do?'

Alanna sat curled in a corner of the sofa, an untouched glass of wine on the table beside her, her throat tight, tension knotting her stomach, as the question echoed and re-echoed in her head.

But always receiving the same answer. 'I don't know.'

For the first time since leaving university, she was unemployed—and scared.

She was also alone, as Susie had agreed to meet an ex-boyfriend for an after-work drink.

'Just a drink, I promise. You will not have to avert your gaze at bedtime.'

Which gave her time to decide on a feasible explanation for leaving Hawkseye so precipitately without too many embarrassing disclosures.

It occurred to her that, although she'd be entitled to a proportion of the current month's salary, she was totally ill-informed about possible benefit entitlement. She hadn't really expected they would ever matter.

At the same time she suspected that her resignation had put her in a bad place to make claims.

She sighed. All this, of course, was something she'd have to find out about.

But it was the immediate future which was troubling her. The last thing she wanted was to find herself dependent on the bank of Mum and Dad, or living at home even temporarily.

However, it seemed clear she could not afford to go on living in London either, and certainly not continuing to share this flat and its expenses with Susie, and she owed it to her friend to tell her this as soon as possible, so she could find someone else.

She hadn't simply lost a job she loved, she thought, biting hard into her lip. Her whole life was falling apart.

And all this because she'd told Zandor she wouldn't sleep with him?

No, not just that, she thought, swallowing past the painful lump in her throat. Because she'd told him over and over again to leave her alone. Insisted that she wanted him out of her life.

Accepted Gerard's nonsensical proposal in order to drive the point home.

And now Zandor had taken her at her word, and she was cut off—stranded in some bleak, unforgiving desert of her own making.

And how stupid did that make her? she wondered drearily.

Almost as foolish as the girl who'd stood in an orchard, fantasising about children playing there, as if they'd somehow been her own, and the man who'd fathered them was standing beside her, holding her in the circle of his arm…

A sob escaped her, as she realised that from the moment she'd woken up in Zandor's bed, she'd been fighting her true feelings. Denying that he was the focus of her every dream, every desire.

Instead telling herself forcefully, insistently that all he'd wanted from her was sex, and she'd be crazy to imagine otherwise.

And perhaps she'd been right, yet it made no difference. Because now, when it was too late, she knew with utter certainty that she loved him and had done so from the first.

Admitted at last that one major reason for running away was the hideous memory that, as she was drifting off to sleep in his arms, sated and glowing, she'd broken the first immutable law of the one-night stand.

Actually said the damning words, 'I love you.'

His lips had touched her hair, but his only reply had been, 'Tomorrow.'

When, no doubt, he would have been kind, she thought bleakly. Unendurably so. Would have let her down lightly, perhaps suggesting another meeting on his return from America, at the same time making it clear that a night's pleasure was no grounds for any kind of long-term commitment on his part at least.

And if she'd expected more…

Maybe a shrug. A suggestion that they should simply enjoy the situation for what it was, while it lasted.

And she'd known, lying there beside him, listening to the messages rampaging through her brain, that, as simply and surely as she needed air to breathe, she wouldn't be able to bear it. That she might break down and cry. Even plead.

And how, after that, could she bear to live with herself?

Well, the answer to that had been, 'I couldn't.' So, she'd left, swiftly and quietly, and, she'd hoped, irrevocably.

Except it was never going to be as easy as that.

She sighed, pushing a hand through her hair. It had been madness to say what she had, and she'd known that for a long time.

Since she'd been at school, in fact, and her literature group had been studying the poetry of William Blake, their opinions divided over the three bleak verses of 'Never seek to tell thy love.'

'He was an idiot to say it,' Susie had declared robustly. 'He spoke too soon and frightened the girl away, losing her to another man in the process. Sheer, lousy judgement.'

'No, he was being honest,' someone had protested. 'Saying what was in his heart, even if it was a mistake. Amazing.'

'For a man perhaps,' Alanna said slowly. 'But if a woman had done the same thing—what then?'

'Easy,' said Susie cynically. 'The guy would have run and twice as fast.'

And I agreed with her, Alanna thought wretchedly. Decided that I was never going to wear my heart on my sleeve, or say the 'l' word until I met the right man, and even then he'd have to say it first—and mean it. Not use it as a ploy to get me into bed.

A perfectly good resolution that I let crash and burn, blurting out the words on a wave of post-rapture euphoria.

I had no guarantees of any kind from Zandor, and why would there be when, as Joanne told me, he has girls everywhere?

Although this Lili seems to be the top of the heap as she might well have been a year ago too.

But maybe she has sufficient nous not to expect too much from a man who can afford anything that life has to offer, she thought, wincing.

But that was never possible for me, because I wanted so much more. From that first moment, I knew I needed to be everything to him.

And now I'm less than nothing, and somehow I have to live with that.

She felt those inner knots of tension begin to unravel and, as the first slow, heavy tears scalded her face and the aching sobs choked in her throat, realised they'd been all that was holding her together.

She didn't even try to stop crying because she

needed the catharsis of tears. Within her, there was a deep well of wretchedness, mixed with remorse and bewilderment, that had to be drained before she could re-start her life.

So, she let the storm of weeping have its way with her, until, finally, there was nothing left.

She sat up slowly, shivering, and drank some wine, feeling it warming her. Signalling she was ready to take control of herself again. Reminding her too that she might soon have to face Susie looking like a drowned rat.

In the bathroom, she relentlessly showered away all traces of grief, and used drops to soothe her swollen eyes before dressing in khaki slouch pants and a black T-shirt.

By the time her flatmate returned some half hour later, she had a pasta sauce bubbling on the stove, sending out welcoming aromas of tomato and garlic.

'Smells almost good enough to eat.' Susie dropped her bag and ditched her jacket with a sigh.

'I thought maybe you'd be dining out.' Alanna took a packet of penne from the cupboard.

'So did I—for about five minutes.' Susie rolled her eyes. 'Listen and learn, dear friend. When something is dead, give it decent burial. The kiss of life definitely does not apply.'

How right she is, Alanna thought, as pain treacherously slashed at her again. She managed to summon a smile. 'I'll try to remember that.'

The meal over, she made a pot of coffee and carried it into the living room.

Susie's brows lifted as she took an appreciative sip of the dark, rich brew. 'A great meal and now the good Colombian blend? *Pourquoi?*'

'I thought we might need it.' Alanna took a deep breath. 'I—resigned from my job today.'

Susie replaced her beaker on the tray very carefully. 'May I ask why?'

Alanna shrugged. 'Because the threatened takeover has now become harsh reality, and I found it was either jump or be pushed.'

'My God,' Susie said blankly. Then: 'What did Gerard say?'

Alanna swallowed. 'I—I haven't actually told him yet.'

In fact, until this moment, I hadn't given him a single thought, she added silently and wished she could summon at least a trace of guilt.

'Worried that he might whisk you to the altar while you're still reeling?'

Alanna bit her lip. 'There's no chance of that. And I've told you first because I'm probably going to run into financial difficulties in the near future and you need to look for another flatmate.'

'While you sleep rough in a doorway, I suppose.' Susie shook her head reprovingly. 'No way, babe, and no arguments either. My trip to the States earned me a good bonus and I can afford to pick up the slack while you find your feet again.'

Alanna said shakily, 'I don't know what to say.'

'Then save your energy for rebooting your CV.' Susie paused frowning. 'What I can't figure is why this new company let you go. Who is it, anyway?'

'Some outfit called TiMar International.' She tried to sound casual.

Susie whistled. 'Is it indeed? As in strong family company turned media and leisure giant in one generation, and still expanding thanks to young dynamic boss. Or that's what they were saying in New York. And now they've moved into mainstream publishing too.' She retrieved her coffee and drank thoughtfully. 'I think I'd have been tempted to hang around for a while. Check out any planned changes.'

'Unfortunately, I found I was to be involved in a really bad one with no alternative,' Alanna said quietly. 'Anyway, perhaps I'm due for a move. A new challenge.'

'Maybe,' Susie agreed doubtfully. She paused. 'But if Gerard offers, promise me you won't take a job at Bazaar Vert, even on a temporary basis.'

'I promise—but why?'

'Because within a week, you'll be crowning someone with an ethnic vase,' said Susie. 'You've been warned.'

'You didn't tell me about my cousin.'

Alanna stiffened. Oh, God, she thought. What can he have heard?

She met his faintly accusatory glance across the restaurant table. 'What do you mean?'

'That he's just bought your publishing house. What else?'

'Oh.' She paused. 'Well, that only happened a few days ago, and I thought you'd already know.'

'Not until I read it in the Business section. In fact, I didn't realise he was still in London,' Gerard said shortly. 'And I certainly never ask about his latest acquisitions or there wouldn't be time to discuss the Bazaar Vert chain, which is my only concern.'

He paused. 'So, how do you like the idea of working for Zandor?'

She bit her lip. 'That's—not actually going to happen. You see—I resigned from my job on Monday.'

He put down his knife and fork. 'But you're bound to serve a period of notice surely?'

'Not on this occasion.' She kept her voice bright. 'I was told to clear my desk and go.'

'Good God, Alanna.' His smile was uneasy. 'Tell me you haven't been embezzling the petty cash.'

'I hope that's a joke. In any case, I wouldn't know how.'

'Then why?'

She shrugged. 'Like a divorce. Irreconcilable differences but with a senior editor instead of a partner.'

'That's ridiculous.' He paused, frowning. 'I'll have a word with Zandor. Get you reinstated.'

'No,' she said too quickly. 'Please don't do that. I—I can find another job. And, anyway, he has better things to do than concern himself with someone at the bottom of the food chain.'

'Not when she's my future wife,' he said shortly. 'And, on that subject, I'm glad to see you're wearing a ring,' he added, studying the glimmer of the opals on her left hand. 'Not exactly what I'd have chosen, but that can be dealt with later.'

The 'future wife' reference sent alarm bells jangling. But now, for all sorts of reasons, did not seem to be the time to tell him once and for all that there'd be no 'later'.

She shrugged again. 'Well, the announcement's been in the papers, and we're having dinner with your Aunt Caroline tomorrow night, so I felt it would be appropriate.'

'Yes.' He was silent while their plates were cleared, and dessert menus proffered. 'It seems that Grandam is staying with her, so it will be a real family party.'

Only if it's the Corleone family, thought Alanna, groaning inwardly. Do I really need this?

She said, 'Does your grandmother often come to London.'

'No, it's usually just for the Horse of the Year show at Olympia.' He looked faintly awkward. 'This time, however, I think she might want to mend a few fences. Discuss dates for meeting your parents, the engagement party and so on.'

Alanna forced a smile. 'In which case, that's what we'll do.'

After some deliberation, she chose a plain shift dress in olive green linen for Saturday evening's dinner. It wasn't a favourite of hers by any means, in fact she was always meaning to give it to a charity shop because it creased at a glance and the colour did little for her, but it was slightly more than knee-length and short-sleeved with a demure scoop neck, all of which should withstand the kind of hostile scrutiny she was expecting.

As if she didn't have enough problems already...

But—one last outing for it, she told herself with a mental shrug as she fixed gold studs in her ears and slid her grandmother's ring onto her finger. And, perhaps, not many more with Gerard.

The Healeys lived in a tall semi-detached house in a street of identical properties. The door was opened to them by an elderly comfortable woman, greeted by Gerard as 'Nanny'.

'Came to look after Des and never left,' he'd confided to Alanna as he parked the car. 'And she does the cooking, so at least we'll get a decent meal.'

Indicating that he viewed the evening ahead with as little relish as herself, Alanna decided with amusement, hoping at the same time that Desmond and Julia might also be there to ease the situation.

But her amusement and her hopes were equally short-lived. As they walked down the hall towards the rear of the house, they heard a high-pitched bray of female laughter, oddly familiar and emanating from the room at the far end.

Glancing at Gerard, she saw his mouth had tightened into a thin furious line and thought, Oh, God—it's Felicity.

She found herself in a large, pleasant room with sliding doors opening onto the garden, golden in the evening sunlight.

And there, like the worm in the bud, was Felicity, stick-thin in ice blue again, this time with ruffles, and ensconced with Niamh Harrington on one of the cream leather sofas which flanked the empty hearth.

She swept Alanna with a look which silently confirmed all her suspicions about the olive dress, then passed on to Gerard, her lips curving into a dazzling smile.

'Hello, my pet. This must be a surprise, but your grandmother absolutely insisted.'

I bet she did, thought Alanna, and just when he thought it was safe to go back in the water...

'Good to see you both.' Richard Healey came over to shake hands. 'Now, what can I get you to drink.'

There was a jug of orange juice on a side table, so Alanna chose that while Gerard asked for whisky and water.

Mrs Healey was also on her feet, fussing about seating, and directing Gerard to the space which had conveniently appeared between Felicity and his grandmother, while indicating that Alanna should sit opposite.

'Now isn't this cosy,' said Niamh Harrington with a stunning disregard for the truth. Her gaze went straight to Alanna's left hand and her brows rose. 'So you have a ring now, dear girl. Well, well, that's a pretty little trinket.' She patted Gerard's arm. 'You've picked yourself a thrifty wife, my lad.'

Which was not intended as a compliment, thought Alanna. Aloud, she said composedly, 'I'm so glad you like it, Mrs Harrington.'

'Oh, not so formal, please.' The blue eyes twinkled at her. 'After all, you'll soon be one of the family, so you must call me Grandam.'

When hell freezes over, Alanna returned silently, at the same time letting her eyes widen in an imitation of shy gratification, which changed to real thankfulness when she heard the chime of the doorbell.

Desmond and Julia, she thought. At last. And looked across, smiling, as the door opened to admit them.

Only to feel the smile freeze on her lips as she saw who was actually standing there.

'Good evening,' said Zandor, and walked unhurriedly into the room.

He was not alone. The girl beside him was spectacularly beautiful, dark-haired and creamy-skinned, her vivid blue eyes shaded by long, curling lashes, her lips the colour of a pale rose. Her dress was pink too, and clung to every inch of an exquisitely curved body.

'Forgive the intrusion, Aunt Caroline,' Zandor went on, his eyes carelessly scanning the surprised faces, flicking past Alanna as if she did not exist. 'But when I heard my grandmother was in town, I felt I couldn't miss an opportunity to bring Lili to see her. After all, it's so seldom they're on the same continent.'

So this is Lili, Alanna thought numbly. The girl who was his personal leader of the pack and who, according to Joanne, he'd been wise not to bring to the abbey. But here now. And, dear God, with him.

She'd thought that Monday's crying jag would somehow have dulled her emotions, setting her on the path to recovery, but as her entire body tensed to resist the pain that slashed at her, she knew that had been a vain hope.

That she was still as hopelessly, helplessly involved as she'd been from the moment she met him.

And the fact she now had the living proof that

she'd lost the battle before it even began made no difference, even though she regretted even more her choice of the olive dress.

And how many kinds of idiot did that make her? she wondered wearily.

'Quite right too, Zan.' Richard Healey breezily filled the astonished and distinctly fraught silence. 'Wonderful to see you again, my dear, and looking lovelier than ever. Isn't she, Caroline? And, of course, you'll both stay for dinner.'

'Yes, indeed,' said Mrs Healey, as if the words were being choked out of her. 'But I wish you'd given us some notice, Zandor. I'm not sure…'

'Nonsense, darling,' her husband interrupted firmly. 'Nanny always over-caters. Besides, salmon mayonnaise and summer pudding stretch anyway.'

'In that case, we'd be delighted,' Zandor said quietly.

He turned towards Niamh Harrington, sitting bolt upright, her face a frozen mask. 'Well, Grandmother.' There was an edge to his tone. 'Aren't you going to welcome Lili—after all this time?'

'Naturally.' Mrs Harrington's voice was level. She extended her hand towards his companion. 'It's good to see you, my dear. Come and give me a kiss.'

As the girl obeyed, Alanna saw Gerard scrambling to his feet, his expression taut, his face dully flushed.

Lili bent gracefully, just touching her lips to

Mrs Harrington's cheek. As she straightened, she also turned. 'Good evening, Gerard.' A soft, husky voice. 'Many congratulations on your engagement. I hope you'll invite me to your wedding—and that you'll also come to mine.'

He cleared his throat. 'You're getting married? I—I didn't know.'

She shrugged. 'It can hardly be a surprise. I thought Zandor would have mentioned it.' Her eyes rested briefly on Alanna who had the odd sensation she'd stopped breathing. 'To all of you.'

Mr Healey interposed again. 'Well, we wish you every happiness, my dear. It's certainly richly deserved. Isn't it, everyone?'

And nodded as a chorus of voices assured him he was perfectly correct in his assumption.

Only Alanna remained silent, not trusting herself to speak as she fought the wave of misery threatening to break over her and sweep her away all over again.

A possibility she could not risk.

Lili's arrival explains so much, she thought wretchedly. His sudden interest in Leahaven Manor for one thing, and my hasty dismissal from Hawkseye for another. Not revenge for rejecting him, after all, but a safety precaution.

But could he really have imagined I'd somehow be tempted to indiscretion? That I could really be that low?

Apparently, he did, and maybe our last encounter gave him good reason to think I was capable of anything.

She washed the bitterness of that away with a gulp of orange juice.

But nothing could erase her dread of the evening to come. Of having to watch Zandor, happy with the girl he'd loved and chosen.

Or of having to desperately pretend that she didn't care, and that she remained the only one who knew that her heart was breaking.

CHAPTER TWELVE

HAD ANY OTHER dinner party in the history of the world ever lasted as long as this one?

Alanna asked herself the question in silent desperation as she struggled to eat from each course set in front of her.

No food, even as delicious as this certainly was, could compensate for the forced conversations, begun then petering out into yet more awkward silences.

Even Niamh Harrington's twinkling buoyancy seemed to have temporarily deserted her and the entire occasion, unlikely to have been more than a muted celebration at best, appeared, somehow, to have turned into a wake.

But why?

Her pseudo-engagement was undoubtedly deeply unpopular—and the sooner it ended the better—but it had been solely Mrs Harrington's idea to invite Felicity, and if Alanna thought for one moment that the other girl had serious feelings for Gerard, she'd have had real sympathy for her.

But she didn't think so, not by a country mile. On the contrary, she believed that Felicity was prompted mainly by self-interest, and this, coupled with Gerard's open indifference, did not bode well for a shared future, even when she herself was finally out of the picture.

But this lack of judgement, bordering on malice, by Niamh Harrington hardly accounted for the air of gloomy uneasiness which permeated the gathering.

And if Zandor's arrival was the cause, why should anyone but herself be affected by his decision to marry his current girlfriend, astonishingly beautiful and clearly known to them all?

After all, despite his wealth, or maybe because of it, he was clearly the outsider in the Harrington clan, so why should they care what he did?

Unless, she thought painfully, her own secret devastation at the news had somehow imparted itself to everyone else, like firedamp spreading, unseen but lethal through an underground tunnel.

But without, God willing, the subsequent explosion.

As for Gerard, he seemed to be immersed in some inner struggle of his own, she noted with bewilderment.

Maybe he thought Zandor's acquisition of Hawkseye Publishing for his media section might be bad news for the Bazaar Vert chain, which could only form a small part of his business empire. Was he worried in case his cousin was planning a sell-off?

Or perhaps he was simply galled that his grandmother had chosen to inflict Felicity upon them again.

Back to square one, she thought. Except he looked far more unhappy than angry, as if some blow had fallen from which he might never recover.

It occurred to her, oddly, that it was the most emotion she'd ever seen him show. That something had shaken him out of his usual pleasant equability.

And, from the one brief glance Alanna had permitted herself in his direction, she'd seen that Zandor also seemed grimly preoccupied while Lili had rarely lifted those brilliant blue eyes from her plate.

Hardly the picture of a happy couple...

Hastily, she closed her mind to that way of thinking, knowing it was more than she could bear.

Perhaps they'd all just stumbled into the evening from hell, she told herself wearily, and were simply trying to deal with it in their own particular ways.

She was startled out of her reverie by the sound of her name, spoken by Niamh Harrington in a cooing tone which automatically prompted her to tense.

'So, you've joined the family twice over, dear girl, now that Zandor apparently owns your little publishing company. How will you like working for him, I wonder?'

Alanna made herself meet the sharp blue gaze with outer tranquillity. 'I'm afraid you've been misinformed, Mrs Harrington. I'm no longer with Hawkseye, so the situation doesn't arise.'

'No longer with Hawkseye?' Mrs Harrington repeated the words meditatively. 'Surely you don't mean you've had the sack?' She rounded on Zandor. 'What can you be thinking of, adding your cousin's intended to the jobless? That's an unkind trick, and her with a wedding in the offing. Can't we all persuade you to think again—be merciful.' And her gaze, once more operating on all cylinders, twinkled round the table.

'No, please.' Alanna felt her skin turn to fire, as this unexpected humiliation bit deep. 'I—I wasn't fired. I actually decided to leave.'

But Niamh hadn't finished with her yet. 'A job you loved.' She frowned as if bewildered. 'But why?'

Zandor spoke, his voice as cold as his eyes. 'I believe she cited personal reasons.' He shrugged. 'Whatever they might be.'

'A little mystery.' Mrs Harrington clapped her hands. 'Don't leave us in the dark, Alanna. Tell all.'

Which she couldn't do, even if she wanted to…

Anger welled up inside her as she forced herself to meet Zandor's brooding, bitter gaze.

She said with icy clarity, 'There's no mystery. Your grandson knows my reasons as well as I do, Mrs Harrington, if not better, and is well aware I really had no choice. And, as that's all I have to say, perhaps we could change the subject, and avoid boring everyone else to death.'

Out of the corner of her eye, she saw Lili move, lean forward, her blue eyes flashing angrily at her, only for Zandor to place a hand on her arm, as if halting any possible accusation in its tracks.

I wonder, she thought, her throat tightening, exactly what he's told her? A full confession of how I threw myself at him? How I told him I loved him? How I went willingly into his arms that afternoon in the orchard?

If so, and I know now how cruel he can be, no wonder she's glaring at me as if I'm her bitterest enemy?

She decided her best plan was to grab Gerard as soon as the meal was over and ask to be taken home, pleading a headache. But when she reached the sitting room where coffee was being served, he'd already been commandeered by his grandmother, and made to join her on the sofa, where she was talking to him quietly and earnestly, drawing an invisible line around them that excluded everyone else.

And especially me, thought Alanna.

She saw Zandor enter the room with Lili, and realising there could still be a scene in the making, headed straight for the open French doors and the lamplit patio beyond.

She paused at the edge of the stone flags to breathe in the cooler evening air, and the aromas of night-scented stocks, lavender and roses reaching her from the shadows of the garden.

She heard a step behind her and turned, instantly

on guard, but it was Richard Healey who was approaching, carrying a cup and saucer in each hand.

'I've brought you some coffee, my dear.' He handed her one of the cups, adding, 'I didn't know if you wanted cream.'

'No thanks.' She could have kissed him. 'Black will be fine.'

'I dare say you need it.' He paused. 'I'm afraid this evening hasn't worked out at all as planned, and I apologise for that.'

'It's hardly your fault.'

'Except I should have put my foot down years ago, when Caroline and I were first married.' His tone was sombre. 'The fact is Maurice and I totally underestimated our mother-in-law's influence over her children, and poor Meg, of course, never stood a chance.

'But one of them fought back.'

She cleared her throat. 'You mean Marianne.'

'Ah,' he said. 'Then you know the story.'

'Joanne gave me the general outline.'

His mouth relaxed into a smile. 'Of course—the family's jungle drum.' He hesitated. 'But did she also tell you about Lili?'

Her throat tightened. 'She—was mentioned.'

'Then, once again, there's no need to say more. Let the past remain in the past, and don't worry about it. Just plan for a happy future.'

He sighed. 'I could wish, of course, that Zandor had chosen another occasion to drop his bomb-shell, but—' his smile became a grin '—on the other hand, I can't deny I enjoyed seeing his grandmother wrong-footed for once.'

Is that what really happened? Alanna asked herself as she drank her coffee, feeling the dark, rich brew putting heart into her.

Zandor's so clearly an outsider that it shouldn't matter to Niamh Harrington if he decides to get married—unless she has another Felicity all picked out for him?

But I can't let it matter to me either. I must let the past remain in the past, just as Mr Healey said, even though I can't foresee a happy future unless it's to know that Gerard will never form part of it.

And as she accompanied Mr Healey towards the house, she sighed soundlessly.

On the threshold of the drawing room, she halted in surprise. Apart from Gerard and his grandmother, the room was deserted but the atmosphere felt like walking into a force field.

Richard Healey paused too. 'Where is everyone?'

Niamh Harrington sat bolt upright, her lips compressed. 'Zandor has gone, and the girl with him, and Caroline is saying goodnight to Felicity, something Gerard here has declined to do.'

'Because I'd have been more inclined to say good riddance,' Gerard returned icily. 'Think of that before you invite her another time.'

Mrs Harrington's pink and white complexion turned a dull red. 'How dare you speak to me like that, Gerard. You forget yourself.'

'Oh, no, Grandam.' He shook his head almost wearily. 'There's nothing wrong with my memory. On the contrary, I wish there was.'

There was a note in his voice that Alanna had never heard before. Something raw and savage.

Something that distracted her from the tormenting image of Zandor and Lili going off together, maybe back to that same hotel to make love in that same bed, and prompted her to intervene, saying quickly and quietly, 'We should be going too. Don't forget we're lunching with my parents tomorrow.'

For an odd moment, they both looked at her as if they had no idea who she was or why she was there, then Gerard seemed to give himself a mental shake, producing a placatory smile.

'Yes, of course, darling. I was wondering where you'd got to. Has Uncle Richard been looking after you?'

'Like a saint.' From somewhere she conjured up a serene smile to direct at Niamh. 'Goodnight, Mrs Harrington. Enjoy the rest of your stay.'

As they drove back to her flat, Gerard still wore a preoccupied air.

Expecting to be dropped off, she was surprised to hear him say abruptly, 'May I come in?'

'Well, yes,' she said, unable to think up an excuse.

'Where's Susie?' he asked, surveying the empty living room.

'In Lewes,' she said reluctantly. 'At her aunt's silver wedding.' She paused. 'Coffee?'

'Fine.'

She ground the beans and was spooning them into the cafetière when he came up behind her, putting his arms round her and turning her to face him.

'Gerard.' Surprised and not pleased, she tried to free herself. 'You've made me spill…'

She was silenced by the sudden heated pressure of his mouth on hers, greedy and probing, while his hands fumbled for her breasts.

For a minute, shock stilled her, then she began to struggle in earnest, her own hands braced—pushing against his chest, until, eventually, she had to reinforce her resistance by bringing her heel down hard on his instep.

Gerard gasped, swore and released her. He stepped back and stood staring at the tiled floor, his shoulders slumped.

Alanna leaned against the counter top, fighting to control her breathing.

She said shakily, 'What the *hell* was all that about?'

'I hoped—us.' He spread his hands almost helplessly. 'Being engaged, for God's sake.'

'But we're not,' she objected. 'You know that. You

asked me for help and I agreed—against my better judgement, and largely because I wouldn't wish Felicity Bradham on my worst enemy.

'But I certainly didn't agree to anything else, and now the whole business is spiralling out of control, just at the moment when even your grandmother must see Felicity as a non-starter.'

'Grandam sees only what she wants,' he said bitterly.

'Then just stand up to her as you did tonight,' she urged. 'You'll be amazed at the support you could get from the rest of the family.'

His voice was weary. 'What's the point of fighting a battle when you know the war's already been lost?'

'Oh, cut the self-pity,' Alanna flung back at him, her raw nerves driving her to exasperation. 'Because in the general scheme of things you're a front runner.'

Ignoring the scattered coffee, she grabbed two beakers from a cupboard, dropped a tea bag into each of them and poured on boiling water.

On her way to the fridge for milk, she began ticking items off on her fingers. 'You're healthy, good-looking, with a great job, a terrific flat and the kind of leisure most people dream about.'

'Yes,' he said heavily. 'And I'd give up all of it if I could only take back the past year. Live it all over again—differently.'

'Wouldn't we all?' she said bitingly. 'Well, dream on, because it's never going to happen. Miss the first bite and you won't get another.'

'Talking of missing out.' He gave her a curious look. 'What was all that business over dinner? Exactly why did you leave Hawkseye?'

Alanna had been expecting this.

'Because I realised I'd just announced my engagement to my new boss's cousin, and I knew someone was bound to make the connection,' she said, with a shrug. 'I figured there were almost bound to be redundancies, and if my name wasn't on the list, things might have got complicated.'

'More than they already are?' he asked ironically, then frowned. 'All the same, it seems an extreme reaction.'

'Not to me,' she returned briskly. 'Believe me, I'm better out of it.'

He said slowly, 'I even wondered if the job meant less to you because you were warming to the idea of marrying me.'

She handed him a beaker of tea. 'No,' she said. Then, more gently: 'No, Gerard, I'm afraid not.'

'Because I want you to know that wouldn't be a problem.'

'But it would almost certainly become one.' She sighed. 'And, right now, I think we have all the difficulties we can handle.'

There was a silence, then he said, 'What happens

now? Does tomorrow's meeting with your parents still go ahead?'

'Yes, of course. We need to keep the pretence going for at least a month or so.' She forced a smile. 'Who knows? By then you may have met someone else.'

'No,' he said. 'I can safely say that isn't going to happen.' He paused. 'And I apologise for earlier.' His smile was rueful. 'I'm not usually the grabbing type.'

She said gently, 'I'm quite sure of that.'

After the tea was drunk, Gerard showed a disposition to linger, and Alanna had to chivvy him out with a brisk reminder that he was picking her up at eleven the next morning.

When at last she was alone, she poured herself a glass of wine from the open bottle of Chablis sitting in the fridge, and curled herself into a corner of the sofa, for a review of the events of the dinner party in their unpleasant entirety.

And, in particular, the extraordinary change that had come over Gerard, who'd embarked quite cheerfully on the evening, without reacting too drastically to the unwelcome appearance of Felicity, probably because he was battle-hardened to his grandmother's machinations.

No, she thought, frowning. It was later that his attitude altered. In fact, looking back, she could see it all stemmed from Lili's announcement that she and Zandor were to be married.

And, at the time, she'd been too wrapped up in her own shock and misery to notice she wasn't the only person in the room to have received a body blow.

But she could see it now. Except…

Gerard? she thought incredulously. *Gerard and Lili?* Surely not. It couldn't be.

Yet she found herself remembering her first evening at the abbey and Joanne's casual remark about Zandor's last-minute arrival. 'I guess we must be thankful he didn't bring Lili.'

It had meant little at the time, but now it gained a whole new significance, taking hold of her mind and gripping like a vice.

Gerard could have met Lili first, and, quite understandably, fallen headlong for her, planning his future life around her.

And then—what? A quarrel?

No, she thought. Probably an intervention.

Lili would have been taken to meet the rest of the family at the abbey, perhaps at Niamh's previous birthday celebration when Zandor had presented her with that copy of *Middlemarch*.

Because he had to have been there, Gerard's boss and billionaire cousin, waiting to be introduced to the newcomer.

Watching her, smiling, the silver eyes travelling over her in lazy, undisguised appraisal.

Just, Alanna thought, as he first looked at me. And did he tell her to call him Zan too, switching them both effortlessly to intimacy?

Was that how it had begun for them—but ended for Gerard?

Maybe the original intention had been simply another brief fling. A discreet interlude of pleasure, without commitment, and no harm done.

After all, they were the rich and the beautiful, she thought wretchedly, taking whatever they wanted from life because they could, then moving on regardless of what trail of devastation they might leave behind them.

It all made sense—and yet...

Had they really hurt Gerard because it was love at first sight and they couldn't help themselves, or was it a rather darker story?

Gerard wasn't a poor man by any means, but in comparison to Zandor, it was no contest.

Something that might well have occurred to Lili, she thought slowly, perhaps suggesting that her amazing looks might have a market value. And on which Zandor might be prepared to pay—with marriage.

Yet if this was so, how could Gerard bear to go on working with Zandor—running Bazaar Vert for him?

That was another piece of the puzzle that didn't fit.

When I found out how Zandor had betrayed me over the Jeffrey Winton deal, I walked away, she thought.

Why hadn't Gerard done the same? Surely the job didn't mean that much to him?

So, there had to be more to it. But how was that possible?

What on earth could be so important to Gerard that he'd allow it to outweigh such a betrayal?

And then she remembered the abbey. Of course, she thought. What else?

She remembered how they'd talked about it on the journey down. The enthusiasm bordering on reverence in his voice. That faint indrawn breath of pleasure she'd heard from him when at last it came into view.

Recalled too things that Joanne had let slip about its finances, and how she herself had clutched at the wrong end of the stick, wanting to believe that Zandor was just a ne'er-do-well battening off his aged grandmother, when in reality it was exactly the opposite. That it was his cash being poured into that historic money pit.

Which put Zandor in a position where he could force Gerard to choose between his heritage and the girl he loved.

'My God,' she said aloud, her voice shaking. 'If so, it's positively medieval. It beggars belief.'

There was also another consideration. Whatever she might think of Niamh Harrington, and many of those thoughts were unutterable, she was still Gerard's Grandam, a woman in her eighties, and the abbey was her home where her children and her eldest grandson had been born, so her wishes and well-being must have been a prime factor in his decision.

Gerard must have been torn apart, she told herself sombrely. And I accused him of self-pity.

At the same time, she needed to remind herself that she had no proof that any of these conclusions were true, even though nothing would ever convince her that Gerard had not been in love with Lili, or that her loss still haunted him.

And what kind of a marriage would she have with Zandor? One of these arrangements where she spent his money and looked glorious on his arm, while turning a blind eye to the way he amused himself when he was away from her?

The thought turned her stomach.

But at least I'll never again be the object of his attentions, she told herself.

The sound of the door buzzer startled her. She was tempted not to answer in case it was Gerard returning in hope of consolation.

On the other hand, it could well be Susie back early from Lewes without her key, so, sighing, she went to the door, unfastening the latch and pulling it open, only to stand in stunned silence as she saw who was waiting in the passage outside.

'So you haven't gone to bed yet,' said Zandor. 'You must have been expecting me.'

And before she could slam the door, he walked past her into the living room.

CHAPTER THIRTEEN

WHEN ALANNA COULD SPEAK, 'What the hell are you playing at?' she demanded huskily.

Hands clenched at her sides, she glared at him, masking with aggression her sudden trembling weakness at the sight of him. 'How dare you force your way in here?'

'It didn't need much force,' he returned coolly. 'Nor am I playing.'

'How did you find me? Get this address?' She bit her lip. 'Oh, your cousin Joanne, I suppose.'

'Then you'd be wrong. Your personal details are still on record at Hawkseye. The company owes you some money. Once it's paid, they'll be removed.'

He glanced around him, appraisingly. 'Nice place. Do you live here alone?'

'No,' she said stonily. 'If it's any of your business. I have a flatmate. She—she'll be back soon.'

'If you say so. Actually, I thought Gerard might be here.' He paused then added deliberately, 'Looking for consolation.'

The sheer cruelty of that made her gasp. 'Do you blame him?'

He shrugged. 'If you make a wrong choice, you pay for it. Something you would do well to remember, my sweet one.'

She said huskily, 'And don't call me that. You—you have no right.'

'No?' His mouth twisted. 'Yet you've been mine, and I found you infinitely sweet. And quite unforgettable, believe me.'

'I wouldn't believe you if you told me today was Saturday.'

He glanced at his watch. 'Which it still is—if only just. But I should have known Gerard had left if only because you're still wearing that awful apology for a dress.'

She flushed hotly. 'I don't dress to please you,' she said curtly.

'Not at the moment, anyway. Or undress either—but I can hope. Don't worry. I shall not insist.'

She stared at him in disbelief. She said thickly, 'My God, you have absolutely no shame, do you?'

'Yes, of course, when it's called for.' His own tone was dismissive, his gaze direct. 'In this case—no.' He paused. 'Won't you ask me to sit down?'

'No.' Alanna marched to the door and held it wide.

'On the contrary, I'm telling you to get out.'

'In my own good time. Meanwhile, why don't we have some coffee.' He walked to the kitchen door and paused, eyebrows raised. 'Except there seems to have been a fight with it. Interesting.'

He picked up the wine bottle, and reached into

the glass-fronted cupboard for a glass. 'I'll share this with you instead.'

She began to feel foolish, standing there stubbornly holding the door open when he clearly had no intention of leaving, so she closed it reluctantly, and came back to sit down again.

She said, 'Where is—?' then found herself stumbling over both *your fiancée* and *your future wife* and chose a compromise. 'Where is Lili?'

'Back at the hotel and, I hope, asleep.' Zandor seated himself beside her, but at the opposite end of the sofa. He sounded, she thought, unforgivably casual.

'Why didn't she come with you?'

'As I said, Gerard might have been here, and I thought it was too soon for that.' He paused. 'I presume he has told you everything?'

She took a sip of wine. 'Enough.'

Well, it wasn't a total lie.

For some reason he'd changed out of the dark suit he'd been wearing at the Healeys' into light chinos and a blue shirt, against which his skin looked like bronze.

Wrenched with longing, she moved further into her corner of the sofa, wondering in self-disgust how she could still entertain such feelings for him, knowing what she did.

Especially when he'd just admitted he'd actually left his lover to come here tonight.

But why?

She took a deep breath. 'Lili—she's very beautiful.'

However much it hurt, she needed to acknowledge that, although it excused nothing and never could.

'I think so.' His sudden smile was warm—even tender, and Alanna winced inwardly. 'In character as well as appearance.'

'Have you told her about—me?' she asked, in spite of herself.

His glance was ironic. 'Enough,' he said, echoing her own earlier response.

She drank some more wine. 'She must be very forgiving.'

'I think,' Zandor said slowly, 'that remains to be seen.'

There was an odd silence which she felt it wiser to break.

'I shall see Gerard tomorrow. We're having lunch with my parents. He—he hasn't met them yet.'

'I see,' he said softly. 'A momentous occasion.'

She flushed again. 'I only mention it because you came here to look for him and you might want me to give him some message.'

'No message.' His mouth curled. 'At least not one you'd wish to carry. And I didn't come here to find Gerard but because, yet again, I have something to discuss with you.

'And don't look so alarmed,' he added coldly.

'This time it's perhaps more business than personal.' He paused. 'At dinner tonight, you seemed to imply that your reason for leaving Hawkseye Publishing involved me. That I'd somehow forced the decision upon you.

'If so, I regret it, and I'm here to ask you to reconsider. To withdraw your resignation and continue your work as a fiction editor, with a rise in salary.'

She stared down into her glass. 'Even when you must know that's impossible.'

'If I knew that, I wouldn't be here. I wish you to return to the company. What prevents you from doing so? Pride?'

'No.' She turned. Faced him defiantly. 'Obviously, a very real fear of sexual harassment.'

Zandor's head went back as if she'd struck him. He said quietly, 'Dear God, is that really what you think? That because I own the company, I'd expect to own you too? Bring my private feelings and desires into the workplace?'

'Your desire for revenge because I rejected you, perhaps?' Her voice shook. 'Then, yes. Why else would you allow me to be—handed over to the unspeakable Jeffery Winton. You were there, Zan, at the bookshop and saw what happened. You— rescued me from him, for God's sake.

'Then, as soon as you took over, you authorised Louis Foster to give me back to him, at his request, to be his own personal editor, presumably because

I'd upset you and knowing full well what it would mean.'

She drew a choking breath. 'And you think anything on earth would persuade me to go back—to that? Let that lecherous little creep anywhere near me again?'

She stopped abruptly, aware there was a danger she might start to cry again, and why that could not be permitted to happen.

Zandor's mouth had straightened into a hard line, and there was a dull flush of anger along his cheekbones.

He said, 'You truly believed that this—order came from me? How is that possible?'

'Louis said "from the top". That's what you'd just become.' She paused. 'And in the staff meeting, you'd hardly looked at me, so I thought I understood why.'

'What did you expect?' His tone was almost savage. 'That I'd walk the length of the room and kiss the life out of you in front of them all? The temptation was there, believe me.'

'Please don't say things like that. You—have no right.'

'Then let's push all of it into some dark place, and turn the key for ever. Is that really what you want? No, don't answer that. Not now when we're both angry.'

He ran a hand through his dark hair, pushing it

back from his forehead. 'However, I swear to you this is the first I've heard about this particular proposition concerning Jeffery Winton. You're saying he actually *asked* for you? By name?'

'I was told so by Louis. Also that my agreement was pretty much my Last Chance Saloon in the publishing world. So—I walked.'

There was another silence, then Zandor said slowly, 'Up to now, the general consensus, presumably excluding Louis Foster, has been that Mr Winton's day is done. That his Maisie McIntyre sales are in serious decline, the new project he's set on will almost certainly crash and burn, and, as he's now out of contract, he should be recommended to look for another publisher.'

He added flatly, 'An option that I shall back all the way, as the fiction department will be informed when it opens for business on Monday.'

He reached across and took the glass from her hand, putting it down with his own on the little table beside him.

His fingers closed round hers, his thumb stroking her palm very gently. 'So, might that persuade you to change your mind and return to Hawkseye Publishing?'

His touch ran through her like a flame, offering, she realised, shivering at some sensual brink, far more than a job. And in that first searing moment, she knew how easy it would be to yield. To turn to him, offering her mouth, her body for their mutual pleasure.

Because it would be mutual. She had no doubt about that. It was there in the way he was watching her, the brilliance in his eyes as they met hers. As they moved down to the vulnerable curve of her mouth, the urgent swell of her breasts against their lacy confines, the line of her thighs under the cling of her dress.

As if he knew that she was melting, scalding with sheer need, just through the movement of his thumb against her hand.

And if it was just a matter of a physical fusion between two consenting adults, temptation might have proved too much.

But for her, it would be once again, as it had always been, an affair of the heart. Acceptance that she wanted all of him, for ever, as she'd done from the first.

And for him, it would be a callous betrayal of the girl who might not be sleeping at the hotel, but fighting her fears of this very situation as she counted the minutes to his return.

And knew she could allow it to happen.

Must stop it now—once and for all—before—dear God—before he took her in his arms. Before his lips touched hers…

She withdrew her hand from his clasp. She said quietly, even steadily, 'No, thank you.'

She heard his sharp indrawn breath, but when he spoke, his voice was equally composed. 'To what? Hawkseye—or me?'

'To both. The first, because I'd like the challenge of a change.' She lifted her chin. 'The second—because I don't share your casual attitude to infidelity.'

He was silent, then: 'I hope this challenging career doesn't involve marriage to my cousin.'

'Because, as you keep warning me, that's doomed?' She made herself shrug. 'Well, maybe. Maybe not. After all, if you had me first, Gerard had Lili, so perhaps that makes us quits.'

He got to his feet so quickly that the table with the glasses went flying. He looked down at her, hands clenched at his sides, silver eyes blazing.

'Now that,' he said in a voice she did not recognise, 'may be unforgivable.' And went.

Alanna got little sleep that night, and Gerard's wan look when he came to collect her suggested he'd suffered in the same way.

Maybe it was for the best, she thought, remembering to transfer the opal ring to her right hand. If they'd shown up at her parents' house looking like the flowers that bloomed in the spring, the fast-approaching irretrievable rift might have lost credibility.

'But you seemed so right together,' was not what she wanted to hear, in spite of its rarity value.

Her mother and father were warm and welcoming as always, but Alanna was aware from the start that a distinct effort was being made on both sides, and admitted silently that, if this had been a real engagement, she'd have been worried.

As it was, Mrs Beckett snatched a quick, private word with her daughter, while Gerard and her husband were outside having a technical discussion on the Mercedes.

'He's very nice, darling. In fact, quite charming. But you will make absolutely sure, won't you? Because I did think…' She halted, flushing a little. 'Although that doesn't matter now, of course. And your happiness is all that matters in the end.'

Leaving Alanna to wonder about what her mother hadn't said on the largely silent drive back to London.

Susie still wasn't back, but Alanna found a message from Joanne on the answering machine. 'Hi, stranger. How about lunch this week and catch up on all the news? I can do Gibby's Place at twelve-thirty on Friday. Call me if you can't.'

No prizes for guessing which particular item of news was at the top of the agenda, thought Alanna. She was tempted to plead a prior engagement, but decided ruefully she'd probably filled her quota of lies for the immediate future.

And maybe there'd be some temporary relief in talking about Zandor's marriage plans—like biting down on an aching tooth.

Maybe…

By the time Friday arrived, she was regretting her decision.

She couldn't stop thinking about Zandor, kept seeing the image of him, the strained lines of his dark face, the hard glitter of his eyes, the contemptuous curl of his mouth. Kept telling herself he'd had no right to look at her like that.

But, equally, she should not have said what she did. Should not have lowered herself to such a cheap, unpleasant jibe. Which she now bitterly regretted.

But when you were torn apart by jealousy and longing, it wasn't easy to behave well, or even rationally.

Unforgivable.

The word had become her constant torment, stinging at her brain.

Yet why did it matter so much now—when he was lost to her anyway?

I don't know, she whispered silently. Only that—it does—it just does.

And if Joanne insists on going over every detail of his relationship with Lili from first meeting to the present day, I'm not sure I can bear it.

She'd been so sure a year ago that she could make

herself forget him and the night they'd spent together. That she could keep slamming mental doors on her memories. Tell herself that 'out of sight was out of mind' and that time and distance would let her heal.

Never—never had she thought that they would meet again—and under such circumstances.

And now, she had to begin again, excising him from her mind, and ignoring the sharp clamour of her senses.

And I will do it, she told herself. Because I must.

She arrived early at Gibby's Place, which was already buzzing, but Alanna was shown to a reserved table by the window and ordered a mineral water while she waited.

I could still avoid this, she thought. Text Joanne that I've had a family emergency and leave.

She was reaching into her bag for her phone, when a girl's voice said, 'Alanna? I thought it was you. I'm so glad to see you.'

She looked up and saw Gina Franklin standing by the table, smiling down at her.

'Gina—what a lovely surprise. How are things?'

'Well, that's why I came over. I'm here with Barbara, the agent you recommended me to. We're celebrating.'

'You've sold the book!' Alanna jumped up and gave the other girl a swift hug. 'I'm delighted for you. I knew it would be snapped up.'

'In the end, there was a kind of auction going on,' Gina said in awed tones. 'I could hardly believe it.' Her face clouded a little. 'But I wish Hawkseye had bought it, so I could still have had you as my editor.'

'I wish so too,' Alanna said with a sigh. 'But it wouldn't have happened. I'm no longer with the company.' She forced a smile. 'Pursuing other interests, as they say.'

'So they were telling the truth,' Gina said blankly. 'You see, I rang Hawkseye earlier to tell you my news, and they said you'd left, but I thought that might be just a way of deterring writing pests.' She shook her head. 'And I thought you were so happy there.'

'I was.' Alanna patted her arm. 'However, things change, just as they've done for you, but not always in a good way.' She became brisker. 'But that's enough about me. Get back to your celebration, and congratulate Barbara for me. You both deserve this.'

At last, some good news, she thought, as she resumed her seat. And now here comes Joanne, probably bringing the direct opposite. And she resolutely pinned on another smile.

'It's so good to see you.' Joanne's hug was warm. 'I gather, as the old Chinese curse says, you've been living in interesting times.'

'So it would seem.' Alanna passed her a menu and subjected her own to an over-elaborate scrutiny, but Joanne was not deterred.

'And Lili's back in London. That must have given Grandam a nasty turn.' She shook her head. 'In fact, it really wasn't her weekend, according to Aunt Caroline, who was on the phone to my mother for a full hour on Sunday morning, pouring out the grisly details.'

She giggled. 'Apparently Uncle Richard's patience has run out, and he was threatening to forbid Grandam the house when Lord Bradham arrived and had the most almighty row with her. Told her she was to issue no more invitations to Felicity. That Gerard clearly did not care for her, and he wouldn't allow his daughter to be humiliated any longer. And that maybe she should have learned her lesson with Marianne who, he realised, had been badgered and manipulated into accepting his own proposal.'

She sat back. 'How about that?'

'And what did Mrs Harrington say?'

'Not much she could say, for once. And, anyway, he didn't give her the chance.

'Following which Uncle Richard weighed in over some of the comments she'd made to you, and half an hour later she was on her way back to the abbey, in the most tremendous strop, declaring she wouldn't be darkening any of her children's doors again, if they allowed her to be insulted like that.'

She giggled again naughtily. 'Dad said he only wished he could believe it.'

She paused to order a salad *niçoise* plus a glass

of the house white, and Alanna, feeling battered, asked for the same.

The wine waiter arrived almost at once, but bearing an ice bucket containing a bottle of Veuve Clicquot and two flutes.

Alanna said quickly, 'There's been some mistake. We didn't order that.'

'No, madam. The ladies who were sitting in the corner had it sent over.' He added, 'And Mrs Fitzcraig also wished me to give you this.' And handed her a business card.

The message on the back read: *I think you'd make a great agent. If you're interested, please call me.* It was signed *Barbara F.*

'Wow,' said Joanne, accepting one of the flutes. 'What's this all about?'

'I think,' Alanna said slowly, 'that I'm being offered a job.'

'Yes, I heard you'd left Hawkseye. Couldn't face having Zan as a boss, I suppose. Yet Gerard seems to have survived, and Lili's done the wise thing and got engaged to some Wall Street prince, so it should be plain sailing from now on.'

She paused. 'Did you happen to hear her fiancé's name? In all the hoo-ha, Mother forgot to ask Aunt Caroline.'

Alanna put her flute down carefully. She said, 'But she's going to marry Zandor. I thought you'd have realised that.'

Joanne stared at her open-mouthed. 'Marry Zandor,' she repeated, then burst out laughing. 'My God, Alanna, are you crazy? I know Grandam regards him as the son of Satan, but even she's never accused him of incest.'

'Incest?' Alanna spoke hoarsely. 'I don't understand.'

'I mean they're brother and sister.' Joanne shook her head. 'Honestly, Alanna, how could you possibly not know that?'

And she relapsed into more peals of helpless laughter.

CHAPTER FOURTEEN

'SISTER?' ALANNA REPEATED the word blankly. 'But Zandor doesn't have a sister. Gerard went all through all his immediate family with me before your grandmother's birthday party and I swear he never mentioned her.'

She paused. 'In fact, apart from you, no one did. And I naturally assumed you were referring to one of Zandor's girlfriends.'

'Well that's Grandam's doing,' Joanne said more soberly. 'For her, Lili was in New York and never coming back, so she simply behaved as if she didn't exist, and I guess we all followed her lead—as usual.'

'Her own granddaughter?' Alanna spread her hands helplessly. 'But why?'

Joanne hesitated, looking awkward. 'Because Lili and Gerard were in love and planning to be married. And Grandam wouldn't allow it. So, they split up and the whole subject became taboo.' She hesitated. 'I suppose Gerard hasn't mentioned that either.'

'Not in so many words.' Alanna moved uncomfortably.

His hidden side, she thought. Oh, Susie, how right you were.

'But I saw how he reacted when she walked into

your aunt's house,' she went on slowly. 'And then she announced she was getting married—and she was with Zandor—and they were obviously close—so...'

Joanne nodded. 'So you put two and two together and made five plus. That figures. And Zan and Lili are pretty devoted, and not just because it's always been the two of them against the Harrington clan. He's quite a bit older than her, and after their parents died, he became her unofficial guardian.'

'She's incredibly beautiful,' said Alanna. 'Why was your grandmother so against the marriage?'

Joanne shrugged. 'Because they're cousins, and Grandam's rules forbade it. I did tell you how fanatical she was about blood lines and good breeding strains, and I wasn't joking.'

'But, if Lili and Gerard really loved each other,' Alanna protested, 'why didn't they simply ignore your grandmother and run off together?'

Joanne sighed. 'Because she made it clear if Gerard disobeyed her, he wouldn't inherit the abbey. She made him choose. The real rock and hard place scenario.'

She frowned. 'But I shouldn't be telling you any of this. After all, you're Gerard's fiancée now, so this is all strictly history. That's obviously what he wants.'

Is it? thought Alanna, her mind still reeling. Somehow I don't think so.

Oh, God, what have I done? *What have I done?*

Food had no appeal, but she forced herself to pick at her frankly delicious salad when it arrived, and help it down with sedate sips of champagne, letting her companion's flow of conversation simply wash over her as Joanne moved seamlessly from her latest boyfriend to a speed-dating session she'd attended—'Just for a giggle, darling, and it was *dire*—' and on to a planned holiday '—an all-girls do in Barbados. Some friends of my parents are lending us a cottage on a beach. Can you imagine?'

And gradually, almost imperceptibly the anguished question in her head changed to *What can I do?*

Gradually a plan began to form, some parts of it easier to achieve than others, but all of it requiring her urgent attention.

On the strength of which she ordered a lusciously dark and alcoholic chocolate mousse from the dessert menu and ate every last spoonful.

Coffee, however, she declined, handing over her half of the bill plus tip.

'It's been great, and we must do it again soon,' she said. 'But I have a busy afternoon ahead.'

'Following up the job offer?'

'Almost certainly,' said Alanna, and decided to dive in at the deep end. After all, she thought, remembering her conversation with Richard Healey, if you have access to a jungle drum, why not beat it?

'But first,' she said, sending Joanne a mischievous smile. 'First, I'm going to break off my engagement to Gerard.'

Because she was in a hurry, she took a cab to Bazaar Vert.

The driver showed no inclination to chat, so she was able to sit quietly and decide what she was going to say.

It occurred to her that she hadn't had much contact with Gerard in the past week. A snatched lunch on Monday, attended by some awkward silences, and a few texts were the sum total.

So he might even welcome her decision, she thought, particularly in view of her rejection of his unexpected advances, which must have made it clear she was going to be no one's consolation prize.

Whatever his reaction, she was well out of it.

Her withdrawal from the agreement was simple enough. Felicity Bradham was also out of his life for good, so they were free to go their separate ways. End of story.

No questioning why he'd omitted Lili from the family tree because that might betray the fact that it mattered to her.

And no querying the choice he'd made either. If he truly preferred that decaying heap of white stone to his living, lovely girl, then Lili was better off without him.

But she now understood the inimical looks from those amazing blue eyes across the dinner table. Lili might now be engaged to another man, but it seemed there was still a residue of pain left over from her previous relationship.

And I know all about that, she thought, flinching as the cab turned into the King's Road.

And from Bazaar Vert, she would go straight to Hawkseye Publishing to find Zandor.

Not from any kind of hope for the future—she'd blown that out of the window pretty well—but to offer him an apology for the misjudgement she'd shown. The assumptions that she'd jumped to.

And then, maybe, she'd find some way of starting over. Building a new life for herself.

There was an odd atmosphere in the shop. She sensed it as soon as she walked in. There was no shortage of browsing customers, yet the staff, usually so attentive, were huddled together, talking quietly.

Alanna walked up to the counter.

She said politely, 'Good afternoon. I'd like to speak to Mr Harrington, if he's free.'

The youngest assistant made a sound like a nervous giggle and received a quelling glance from the manageress.

She said, 'Perhaps you'd come with me to the office, Miss Beckett. I'm afraid you've found us rather at sixes and sevens.'

A unique admission for a business that normally ran like clockwork, thought Alanna, but she followed the older woman to the office and watched, bewildered, as she gave an almost deferential knock before opening the door.

'Miss Beckett,' she said. 'For Mr Harrington. I—I didn't know what to say.'

'That's all right, Mrs Trevor.' To Alanna's astonishment, Zandor rose from behind Gerard's desk and walked towards her. 'I'll explain to Miss Beckett.'

Mrs Trevor nodded and backed out, closing the door quietly. Shutting them in together.

But it shouldn't be like this, Alanna thought desperately. I need to see Gerard first—to end this pretence once and for all.

Aloud, she said, 'Where is he? Has something happened?'

He pushed a chair forward. 'Why don't you sit down?'

'No,' she said. 'Whatever it is, just tell me. Has—has there been an accident?'

'Nothing like that.' His eyes went to the opal ring on her left hand. Rested there. 'He's just not going to be around for a while.'

'You've fired him?' She swallowed. 'Because of what happened with Lili?'

'On the contrary.' He paused. 'He and Lili have gone away together, God knows where. Apparently they intend to get married by special licence. She left me a letter this morning.'

For a moment, she felt stunned. 'But she's engaged to someone in America—isn't she?'

'She was.' His mouth twisted. 'There's a letter for him too. Of course, I also have the privilege of telling the family, after which all hell will probably break loose.

'But, with my usual selfish lack of consideration, I decided to sort out Bazaar Vert first. Get a new director in from the Paris branch and make sure it's business as usual. After all, people's livelihoods depend on it.'

He paused. 'And then I was coming to find you.'

'Yes.' She added slowly, 'After all, you did warn me it would never happen—Gerard and me.'

'You think I was coming to gloat?' He shook his head wearily. 'God, Alanna, you've been let down too.'

The initial shock had worn off, leaving her with the sensation that a great weight had been lifted from her shoulders.

She said, 'That's not true. Zandor, there was no real engagement. He just wanted me to pretend—to provide him with a temporary barricade against the Felicitys of this world. I was going to refuse, but then he jumped the gun with that announcement, so I—went along with it. Something I've regretted ever since.'

She smiled. 'But about an hour ago I heard Felicity was no longer a problem, so I came straight here to tell him it was over. Only he's saved me the trouble.' She transferred the ring to her other hand. 'Therefore my grandmother's trinket can go back where it belongs.'

She paused. 'And then I was coming to find you.'

His gaze was steady. 'May I ask why? Have you rethought the job offer?'

'Oh, no. There's a possibility I might become a literary agent instead.'

She took a deep breath. 'I wanted to see you—to apologise. For things I've said—the way I've behaved. It's no excuse, but until an hour ago, I truly believed that you and Lili were—lovers. That the two of you were going to be married, yet you had no intention of being faithful. And I—I couldn't bear it.'

He said slowly, 'That must have been a hell of an hour.' He paused. 'Let me understand this. Are you saying Gerard never told you about my sister—about what happened between them? Or that she even existed?'

She shook her head, staring down at the carpet. 'Not a word. And nor did anyone else. And I—I jumped to all sorts of stupid conclusions—and stayed with them, until today when I had lunch with Joanne, and she told me everything. And now I need to tell you that I'm so sorry.'

There was a silence, then Zandor said, quite gently, 'I'm afraid—I'm definitely afraid that's not enough. And this is a conversation that should be continued elsewhere.'

'No,' she said, dry-mouthed. 'Really. You have enough to do. And I've said all I meant to say.'

'I hope that's not true. In any event, it's now your turn to listen to me.'

He took her arm, steered her to the door and out into the shop.

She tried to hang back. 'Zandor—no. Please.'

'You'll come with me,' he said. 'Even if I have to carry you—and provide the staff with another sensation.'

'But where are you taking me?'

'Isn't it obvious?' They emerged onto the pavement, and he hailed a taxi. 'We've wasted enough time, so we're going back to where it all began, and where it should have continued. You and me. Together—for ever.'

In the cab, he held her hand all the way to the hotel, and she could feel him trembling.

She was shaking too, with fear, excitement and the first stirrings of hope as the lift carried them up to the penthouse.

The suite looked exactly the same—as if the intervening months with their loneliness and misunderstandings had never existed—but she knew it couldn't be as simple as that.

She stood, facing him, in the middle of the sitting room. 'You said you wanted to talk. I'm listening.'

'I need you to answer a question. That night—as you were falling asleep—you said, "I love you."'

He flung his head back, the silver eyes anguished. 'Alanna, I have to know if you meant it, or if it was just the sex talking. Because when you ran out on me that seemed the only explanation I could come up with. At the time I just lay there, holding you, suddenly believing in the age of miracles. Telling myself that you'd thought—that you'd known beyond all doubt, as I did when I first saw you—that here was the one. The only one.'

A muscle moved in his jaw.

'And that when I kissed you awake in the morning, you'd say it to me again—and smile. Only it didn't happen. So, tell me—please—why did you go?'

She said with difficulty, 'Because I was confused—even scared by the way I felt about you. And though what happened had meant the world to me, for you it might just have been another one-night stand. And I—couldn't bear that.

'After all, I'd thrown myself at you and followed up by totally putting my heart on my sleeve, and I couldn't risk you pitying me for me for making a fool of myself when you told me it was over,' she ended with a little gulp.

'And I didn't just walk away. I ended up a total

mess, and told myself I deserved it. That I should be ashamed, going to bed with a stranger. Risking pregnancy. The same thing had happened to a girl I knew, and it had damaged her life for ever.

'In reality, I suppose I was going through a grieving process. And when I met your cousin, it seemed at first like a way back to normality. As if I'd been given some kind of reprieve.' She tried to smile. 'When in fact, we were two messes together.'

He said quietly, 'Did you sleep with him?'

She gasped. 'No—of course not. I could never...' She stumbled to a halt. 'That sounds terrible.'

'A little,' he said. 'For the first time today, I almost sympathise with him.'

He paused. 'I had no intention of going to my grandmother's party, until I heard from Joanne that Gerard was taking his new girlfriend, and that she was called Alanna and had something to do with books. After that, you couldn't keep me away.'

He gave her a straight look. 'That first night at the abbey—you must have known I'd come to you. Why did you lock your door?'

'For that very reason.'

Zandor shook his head. 'Big mistake, my darling.'

'No,' she said. 'For me—a question of survival. Never seeing you again was the cornerstone for the new life I was trying to build.'

'But if you'd let me in, there'd have been no misunderstandings because I'd have told you everything, before or after our blissful reunion, including my well-founded suspicions that Gerard still loved Lili and always would. Then in the morning, we could simply have left for London and a new life together, thus cementing my position as black sheep of the family,' he added ruefully.

'But you can't want that.'

He shrugged. 'It was inevitable. My grandmother hated my father, regarded him always as the scum of the earth, although she had no scruples about taking money from him when the occasion arose. I'm my father's son, so her dislike has been part of my inheritance. Coupled with the illusion that I'm also her private banker.

'And Lili, of course, was my father's daughter, so the real reason Niamh moved heaven and earth to split up her relationship with Gerard had nothing to do with their being cousins, as popularly supposed, but because she couldn't bear to think of my sister, a Varga, as mistress of Whitestone Abbey.'

'Well, she'll have to bear it now.'

'I doubt it. My guess is that Gerard and Lili will move to Paris or even New York. He can still operate as Bazaar Vert managing director from either, if he wishes. But he's finished with the abbey.'

She said, 'It's certainly caused enough trouble. But why did your sister take him back—after the way he'd treated her?'

'Because she loves him and always will.' His

voice was gentle. 'It's as simple as that. Which reminds me.'

He disappeared to the bedroom, and returned almost at once carrying a small box.

He drew her down beside him on the sofa. He said, 'In spite of everything, I was absolutely convinced that we'd meet again, and that this time I was going to be ready. So while I was in New York, in spite of feeling battered and bruised, I bought you this. To keep the faith.'

On a bed of black velvet, the enormous solitaire diamond on its platinum band radiated light and fire.

'We could go on rehashing all the past mistakes we've both made until the end of the world. But I'd rather live in the present and the future. With you.'

He took her hand, and slid the ring onto her finger.

'Marry me, Alanna. Take the risk. Be my wife and make my life worth living again.'

She said, 'I love you.' And lifted her face for his kiss.

'And I,' he said, 'love you, more than life itself.'

A long time later, lying in bed in his arms, totally fulfilled and gloriously weary, she said drowsily, 'God knows what my parents are going to say.'

'Well, we'll soon find out. I thought we'd drive down tomorrow, so I can do the right thing. Ask your father's permission, while you and your mother figure out the when and where of the wedding.

'Anyway, they may not be too surprised,' he added. 'I don't think they really bought into my asking for directions story.'

'No,' she said, remembering something her mother had almost said. 'Perhaps not.'

'And while we're down there,' he went on, 'maybe we could have another look at Leahaven Manor. I had this picture of us there—a family. Crazy perhaps, but…'

She turned her head and kissed his throat. 'Then we're both crazy,' she whispered. 'Because I had the same picture. And it's wonderful.'

*****

If you enjoyed
THE INNOCENT'S ONE-NIGHT
CONFESSION
why not explore these other stories
by Sara Craven?

THE INNOCENT'S SHAMEFUL SECRET
THE INNOCENT'S SINFUL CRAVING
INHERITED BY HER ENEMY
SEDUCTION NEVER LIES

Available now!

Get 2 Free Books,
Plus 2 Free Gifts—
just for trying the Reader Service!

Get 2 Free Books,
<u>Plus</u> 2 Free Gifts -

just for
trying the
*Reader
Service!*

STRS17R2

HOME *on the* RANCH

YES! Please send me the **Home on the Ranch Collection** in Larger Print. This collection begins with 3 FREE books and 2 FREE gifts in the first shipment. Along with my 3 free books, I'll also get the next 4 books from the Home on the Ranch Collection, in LARGER PRINT, which I may either return and owe nothing, or keep for the low price of $5.24 U.S./ $5.89 CDN each plus $2.99 for shipping and handling per shipment*. If I decide to continue, about once a month for 8 months I'll get 6 or 7 more books, but will only need to pay for 4. That means 2 or 3 books in every shipment will be FREE! If I decide to keep the entire collection, I'll have paid for only 32 books because 19 books are FREE! I understand that accepting the 3 free books and gifts places me under no obligation to buy anything. I can always return a shipment and cancel at any time. My free books and gifts are mine to keep no matter what I decide.

268 HCN 3760 468 HCN 3760

Name	(PLEASE PRINT)	
Address		Apt. #
City	State/Prov.	Zip/Postal Code

Signature (if under 18, a parent or guardian must sign)

Mail to the **Reader Service:**

IN U.S.A.: P.O. Box 1867, Buffalo, NY. 14240-1867
IN CANADA: P.O. Box 609, Fort Erie, Ontario L2A 5X3

HRCBPA18

READERSERVICE.COM

Manage your account online!

- Review your order history
- Manage your payments
- Update your address

> ### We've designed the Reader Service website just for you.

Enjoy all the features!

- Discover new series available to you, and read excerpts from any series.
- Respond to mailings and special monthly offers.
- Browse the Bonus Bucks catalog and online-only exclusives.
- Share your feedback.

Visit us at:
ReaderService.com

RS16R